Maggie Goes To Hollywood

Maggie MacKay: Magical Tracker

Book Six

by KATE DANLEY

This is a work of fiction. All of the characters, organizations, and events portrayed in this novel are either products of the author's imagination or are used fictitiously.

DEDICATION

To Adam Jackman
and
every P.A. who has ever make a coffee run

CHAPTER ONE

I woke up to the sound of my phone ringing. Blearily, I peeled open my crusty eyes and tried to read the clock. 2:00 a.m. No good ever comes from answering the phone at 2:00 a.m. A part of me wanted to pretend this time could prove the exception, but the odds were not in my favor.

"Killian, get that, would you?" I mumbled into the pillow.

I felt the bed shift as Killian snuggled against me. "You get it."

It took me a moment to remember what happened last night.

Killian is my partner... erm.... was my partner at M&K Tracking. He's a six-foot-something, ridiculously good-looking wood elf who, up until yesterday, was my go-to guy whenever I needed someone to hold my gun. But circumstances dictated that we close up shop at M&K Tracking and close it quick-ish. So, that's how things started.

We began by packing up Killian's apartment. About an hour in, I explained to him that moving tradition dictated pizza and beer for the helpers. That resulted in him informing me that it was ancient elfin custom to provide fruity ambrosia concoctions as a goodbye gift to the movee. We decided it was high time for a little cultural exchange between our peoples.

So, after we finished all the beverages in the building, we decided to take our 'cultural exchange' to the streets and proceeded to have ourselves what I liked to call an itty bitty bender.

Killian snuggled in closer and I heard the crunch of a paper parasol he still had tucked behind one ear.

I'm pretty sure someone may have slipped us some witches' brew because, seriously, after the fifth or sixth bar, all I remember was Killian and I stumbling into his apartment below M&K Tracking and... passing out simultaneously.

What?

You thought we hooked up?

Do you even know me?

I pushed him away. "Ugh, get off me!"

Fucking elf.

My name is Maggie MacKay. A few days ago, Killian and I were caught up in a plot to destroy... oh, everything. The bad guys were hell-bent on destroying everything. It started with Vaclav and his vampires and their usual plot to tear down the border between Earth and the Other Side so that they could come over for a midnight snack whenever their tummies got rumbly. Blah blah blah.

But THEN we discovered there had been an even bigger bad out there gunning for us. The group was called the Bringers of Light and THEY were intent on breaking down the border between the Dark Dimension and the Other Side, too. Their plan involved getting rid of the elves. Not exactly sure why, but some pointy-eared bug had crawled up their butt. I gotta say, prior to working with Killian, I probably would have signed up to play for their team myself. I mean... fucking elves... But the fae-folk of the forest weren't half bad once you figured out how to put up with them.

That said, the Bringers of Light were assholes. Sneaky assholes. Last year when my dad was still in the business, he and I hauled in a politician who was on vacation with a medusa. Said politician's brother was a snore named Stan who took over as president of the World Walker association. You'd think someone that boring would cause everyone to fall asleep prior to being able to organize a political coup, but Stan started throwing the World Walkers into prison and then used his brother's lady love, said medusa, to turn the World Walkers into statues. Even worse, Stan pulled my permit.

The World Walker Association supposedly hired an angel (who was no angel) named Graham to haul me in. But really, Graham was working for Stan and the Bringers of Light. Sounds like a bad doo-wop group. But Graham tricked me and Killian —okay, just me… I was the only one who fell for it—Graham tricked ME into smuggling an artifact from Earth to the Other Side. This artifact was capable of opening a permanent portal to the Dark Dimension. And, because I didn't know any better, I gave it to the Queen of the Elves. She went batshit crazy and almost killed my partner. We cock-blocked that fuckup, but now, the queen was trapped in a state of suspended animation, and it was up to me and Killian to figure out how to shut down the power of the Dark Dimension stone without killing her.

The ecosystem of the elfin forest was unimpressed by the queen existing in a grey-area when it came to the black-and-white question of living and dying. Unfortunately, the elves are a little like honeybees: when the queen is not queening and time passes without a replacement in the ranks, the elves go to shit. The Mother Tree's roots were rotting without the Queen's life force. The remaining elves were like asthmatics being forced to run in the smog. Killian and I were going to have to break up the business

3

so that he could save the elfin race as best he could while I tried to figure out how to unfuck the fucked-up-ness. It was bad times all the way around.

But not as bad as a phone that would not stop ringing at 2:00 a.m.

"I want to hire you, Maggie," Killian groaned. "Kill the phone. Kill it. I will personally open the treasury of the elves to get you to impale it with any stake of your choosing."

Yawning, I hauled myself out of the bed and shuffled my way across the cold floor. Past Killian's elfin boots. Past my elfin boots. Past my leather coat. Past... Killian's tights?

I paused. "Killian?" I asked. "Are you wearing tights?"

"They bind."

Normally, this would have been just cause to rework the office dress code policy, but we were closing up shop. And I was too hung-over to care. I shuffled on.

Killian had a dining room table made from tree roots he somehow convinced to grow like furniture. I found my phone there, next to my keys and weaponry.

This apartment actually used to be a vampire lair, but Killian had transformed it into his own little glen-away-from-elfin-glen, for those times when we had a long night at the office. Or a long night out-of-the-office. The ceiling looked like the August sky and he had plants everywhere. Something about life force being a good defense against the undead. I found pointy things to be a better option.

I picked up the phone. "Hello?"

"This is the Other Side Police Department. Are we speaking with Margaret MacKay?"

They used my formal name. This was not good.

"Speaking," I said, wishing I was in better fighting form.

"There has been a break in at 451 Midsummer Road. Is this your place of residence?"

I sat down hard on one of the dining room stumps. I guess from the look on my face, Killian figured out something was going down. He kicked off the sheets and stumbled my direction. I guess at some point he had switched into a long, white, man-nightie. He looked like he could go on as Ebenezer Scrooge in a burlesque version of A Christmas Carol.

"That's my house," I replied to the dispatcher as Killian began dispatching some coffee.

"Were you planning on returning to your home tonight?" the guy asked.

"No, I'm out of town," I lied. A) I was in no condition to drive anywhere. B) I was in no condition to fight the forces of evil anywhere. "I'll be there in the morning."

"Huh."

I heard a little shift in his tone, like he was running through the scenarios of why a girl like me wasn't headed home straight away with this sort of news.

"I'm working," I added.

"Right. Working," he replied with what, if I was not mistaken, was a hint of disbelief. "We'll leave an officer to keep an eye on things. Give us a call tomorrow and we'll work with you to catalog what seems to be missing."

I hung up the phone and tossed it on the table. The noise of it clanking was enough to cause both Killian and me to wince.

"What was that in regards to?" Killian asked, putting the cup of coffee in front of me.

I swallowed down the bitter nectar of life force rejuvenation and let it roll down the back of my throat. Probably once I woke up, I'd be more upset, but for now, the robbers could have whatever it was they were looking for and the rest of my Other Side-ly belongs, too, if it meant my head would stop throbbing. "Break in at my house," I said.

At once Killian was at the ready. I wish I had the ability to shake off the effects of a hard night the way the elves could. "Should we go there now?" he asked.

I shook my head and wiped my face with my hands, wishing Killian would use his indoor voice. "And do what? Damage has been done."

"I cannot believe someone would even attempt to burglarize your home," he replied, pouring himself some orange juice. Hair of the dog. I raised my coffee mug in admiration as he continued on. "Do they not understand who you are?"

"Idiots," I replied. "Good thing I'm a tracker, huh?" I laughed without humor. "We'll head over tomorrow, I'll catch their scent, and dispense a little justice MacKay style, preferably when the sun is up and they are fast asleep in their tidy little crypt."

"Unless that is exactly what they want you to do..." said Killian slowly, his eyes narrowing as he sipped from his cup.

"What?"

He set down his glass and leaned against his kitchen counter, arms folded. "Someone—"

"I'm pretty sure, if I remember correctly from getting ambushed in the elfin woods and fighting an undead dragon, that it was vampires."

"SOMEONE," Killian continued giving me a glare to shut my trap while he noodle this thought through out loud. "Stole from my people to draw the Shadow Elves out in order to slaughter them. What if whoever did this wanted to draw you out in order to slaughter you?"

The elf, in addition to looking too good for 2AM and sobering up too good for 2AM was entirely outthinking me too good at 2AM. "Perfect timing is perfect, isn't it?" I remarked.

"We have a lovely evening on the town, which one could assume would have rendered you... perhaps not at your strongest..."

"Delicately put," I said, taking another sip of the coffee to try to get my brain up to working speed with the elf.

"If you were at home, you might have been caught unaware. Or if you were still at the height of our revelry, you may have returned home and then gone... how do you humans put it... with your 'guns a-blazing' to extinguish this evil?"

"Very likely."

"And you may have followed them, hoping to catch them before they could go too far. But neither of us would have been in a state for defending ourselves."

"Lucky for us, we passed out."

"Excellent preemptive strategy."

Killian and I clinked glasses.

"Will you be able to track the perpetrator if we wait until morning?" enquired Killian.

"Oh, ye of little faith." I replied. "It takes more than a couple hours to hide from a MacKay."

Killian looked at me with his baby blues and his eyes got all sad and crinkly around the edges. "Unknown forces infiltrated your home, and whether they were intent on taking advantage of our absence or our state of inebriation, you must pay more attention to your surroundings in future days," he warned.

"I should?" I repeated incredulously to make sure I heard him right.

A little worry line appeared down the middle of his Botox-perfect brow. "I am not going to be here, Maggie," he reminded me gently.

Aw, it was like a punch in the teeth, and a punch in the teeth at 2AM when you're hung-over is especially cruel. I looked around Killian's apartment and wondered who was going to take care of all his plants while he was gone. If it wasn't some sort of a trap, then whoever broke into my house was looking for something, and if they didn't find what they were looking for, the office would be next on the list. And Killian wouldn't be around to help me sweep up the broken glass. The sucky thing about learning to rely on someone is that you forget how it used to seem normal to do things all by your lonesome. I tried to remind myself that I was a one-woman-band long before Killian showed up with that lousy job that started this whole mess.

But I was going to miss the dumb lug.

I sighed, getting up to rinse out my dumb mug. He was right. I DID need to start paying more attention, get back to that place where I knew no one had my back, except me. It's a lot easier to be pleasantly surprised when someone shows up to help rather than to be crushingly disappointed when everyone fails you.

I squished all those thoughts deep into the crevasses of my skull where I wouldn't have to look at them too hard. Right now, there was stuff to deal with.

I turned on the tap and waited for the water to run warm. "You think someone in the bar was watching us?" I asked.

"We went to seven bars, Maggie."

"You think that someone in the seven bars was watching us?"

"Other than everyone?"

Killian was right. Between Vaclav's grudge and the World Walker Association now in the clutches of evil, there was not a single place I could go on the Other Side where someone wasn't keeping tabs on me. The only reason I hadn't been hauled in was that I threw Graham, the fallen 'angel', into the slammer first. He was probably the only bounty hunter with the skills to bring me down. That and whenever the bad guys figured out some scheme to put me away, I got sprung by Lacy, everyone's favorite prison intake officer.

"Well, my place is warded, so it wasn't vampires," I reasoned.

"That is encouraging."

"Which means those Bringers of Light bastards are most likely behind it."

"It would seem logical," said Killian, coming over to

8

take the mug out of my hands and dry it.

"How the hell do we protect ourselves from a loony cult of doomsday activists?"

He wiped the cup out thoughtfully. "Go on a vacation and allow the vampires to eat them?"

"Not such a bad plan," I replied, grabbing his OJ glass. "Remind me to give you a raise."

"How about some paid leave, instead?" asked Killian.

"I love you, Killian," I said. "But not that much."

CHAPTER TWO

I pulled my car up in front of my house. I bought this Arts-and-Crafts style bungalow a while ago with some spare cash, back when such a thing actually existed in my life. A real estate witch had plucked the image out of my head and caused the house to appear just as I had always imagined it. I loved my little house.

And seeing it busted up sucked.

Last night, it all seemed sort of surreal and distant. Now, the glass smashed out of the front window and the police-issued spell tape surrounding the property was bringing the reality of the situation home, so to speak. I slammed the car into park and yanked up the brake with a little too much force.

The only comfort was my psychic-sensitive mother hadn't called in hysterics, which meant this was a mere bump in the road, not some game changer. Or she and my dad were off vacationing in an alternate dimension that had lousy cell service. Both were entirely possible, so I was back to no comfort.

There was a guard goblin sitting on my porch, which was a good sign. It meant someone on the police force still had my back. I got out of my car and walked through the spell tape, feeling it close itself behind me. Spell tape creates a fairly impenetrable bubble around a crime scene ('fairly', because come on, it's government work.) Only those special VIPs listed as "safe to enter" can come in.

But something didn't feeling right…

I stepped into the front yard and gave the goblin a wave. "Hey! I'm the homeowner."

The goblin's buggy eyes narrowed into slits as he observed me. His pointed tongue slithered out from his under bite to lick an offending booger from his gray-green nose. He yammered something at me in goblinese and then scurried away on four legs to do something. I assume to call his superiors to let them know I was around and ready to start cataloging things.

I watched his dog-like body trot out to his patrol car, open the door, and climb inside. He held a phone up to the side of his helmeted head. My red flags were still going up but I had absolutely no idea what was making me feel so ooked.

I didn't need to bother unlocking the door. The dead bolt had been destroyed by someone kicking their way in. From the psychic imprint it left behind, it felt more a police boot print than a burglar boot print. Guess the coppers figured if someone was inside, there was a reason they weren't answering the door.

The only person I cared about was my cat.

"Mac?" I called, looking around for his fluffy, orange form. I knew I'd have felt it if anything bad happened to him, but he was usually there to greet me with a friendly 'brrrrow'. Considering that his full-time job was sleeping in a sunbeam, with occasional temp work hunting down any imps setting up shop in my garden, the absence of 'brrrrow' was not cause for concern, but I knew I'd feel better once I found him.

The house had been tossed. From the ratio of smashed vs. missing objects, I got the sense that their mission was more of a psychological one. While I wasn't particularly fond of strangers getting their grubby paws all over my stuff, the fact they wanted me quaking in my boots made me mad rather than a-skeered. I don't quake for anyone, much less a bunch of asshats who think messing up my shit is all it takes to put the fear in me. I wasn't going to cower on principle. I'm ornery like that.

Still, it sucked to see picture frames cracked and the fabric on the sofa slashed. I fucking loved that sofa. I touched the tear. Three rips started wide and then drew in towards the bottom. So, I was dealing with a clawed, three-fingered monster. Four if it had a thumb. But at least that eliminated werewolves. Had to be a living creature, because the undead wouldn't have been able to get past my wards.

I found the same three-clawed mark running along the length of the wall and up the stairwell. It was going to be stupid expensive to get it patched up. They don't exactly do homeowner's insurance on the Other Side. There's no profit, what with all the monsters roaming around these parts.

In the bathroom, the mirror was smashed and my towels were crammed in the toilet. Well, now I was going to HAVE to move. I hoped whoever did it got the whole seven years bad luck. I still didn't see that they had taken anything.

More importantly, though, I wasn't getting a clear sense of what sort of creature it had been. It felt like something with a big stride, and yet, as I examined the wooden jams, this something was small enough to get through a doorway without crashing their shoulders into it. That ruled out bugbears. Most of the damage was done around waist-high level, with occasional damage above, like it was a shorter, jumpier creature.

I went into my office. The futon inside had been ripped to shreds like someone with knives for hands had bounced on it, and the frame was broken. A week ago, I had thought to myself that it was time for my office to stop looking like a frat boy's dorm room. Now it looked more like a frat boy's dorm room after the best night of his life.

Sometimes the universe does for us that which we cannot do for ourselves, and sometimes that's sending a squad of short, jumpy, knifey creatures on a mission to intimidate and redecorate. Either way, I was getting new furniture.

The wall panel to my armory had been pulverized, but the door held, just like it was supposed to. Everything would be in automatic lockdown, which sucked, but I was glad to know no one was spicing up Sunday dinner with my secret stash of Whole Witches' All Organic Garlic Heads. That shit is expensive.

I walked into my bedroom and it wasn't really that bad. Looked like, from the broken window, this was where my burglar made his exit when the police showed up and spoiled his party. I added "ability to jump out of two-story windows" to my clue list.

I heard a little meow from under the bed and I pulled up the dust ruffle. Mac stretched out his orange paws and yawned at me.

"Nice sleep?" I asked him dryly. "You're slacking on your attack cat duties."

I reached underneath the bed and dragged him out. He was none too happy with me and tried to turn his body into a lead weight. I've taken down trolls with less body mass than my cat, but I managed to pull him out. I held him in my arms and scratched under his chin. He responded by booping me with his head and then trying to eat my hair. I looked out the window at where my perpetrator had escaped. There were four large footprints in the ground where he had landed.

"So what's waist high, got four legs, but can get up on two long enough to tear down my sheetrock, and can jump out of a second story window without breaking said legs?"

13

I murmured into Mac's fur.

Outside, I watched the police-goblin crawl out of the police car onto his all-fours and leap-run to the door of my house, his loping form eating up the distance.

"Oh," I said. "Goblins."

So it turns out that maybe my burglar ate my police officer or maybe my police officer was actually the burglar and this was a setup or maybe a doppelganger ate a goblin and replaced his body with a look-a-like, but whatever the fuck was going on, that goblin was coming back, my armory was in lockdown, and things were fucked.

Mac heard the noise of the goblin running into the house and scrambled out of my arms.

Screw the world. I needed to save my cat.

CHAPTER THREE

"Gawddamnit, Mac!" I shouted, rushing out after him. "Stop running away from me when I'm trying to save you! If you get yourself eaten by a goblin I swear by everything holy I will pass him the ketchup."

For the record, I would never pass a goblin ketchup.

So. Goblins. They are living. They have fairly thick hides, but aren't impossible to defeat. Best to go at one with an ax or a mace, both of which were now in lockdown in my other room. Fantastic. All I had was my gun and my stake, both of which were relatively useless. Goblins are like old leather. A bullet just sort of bores through them, like an awl making a hole. You need something that'll do some large-scale physical damage. I wished Killian was around with his famous collapsible stick.

I looked around the room to improvise. The goblin had taken all this time to call someone from the car and I didn't want to be around when the reinforcements arrived. My phone started ringing in my pocket. It was Wagner's Flight of the Valkyries, a special tune I had assigned for when my mom was calling. If she was phoning, it meant she had felt what was about to happen, and that wasn't good. If I survived it, I'd also have to survive her interrogations. Neither outcome was particularly makin' my day.

I had a baseball bat under the bed. It wasn't perfect, but it was going to have to do in this pinch because I could hear the goblin nearing the bedroom door. Up until now, his crashing around downstairs sounded more like standard-level police-goblin crashing rather than murderous death-hunt crashing, so I think he thought that I still thought he was a good guy. Goblins also aren't exactly the brightest.

He opened the door, saw me with the bat, and came at me with his claws. That was three fingers and a thumb, just as I had deduced, for anyone interested in goblin anatomy. I stood sideways and swung at him like a hitter at the Multi-World Series.

Now, while not the hardest Other Side creature to dispatch, Goblins aren't a cakewalk, either. Goblins are a dirty business. They move fast and can use their momentum to climb up walls. My arm vibrated in my shoulder socket as the baseball bat connected with his jaw.

It threw him backwards and he struck the hall like Wile E. Coyote at the bottom of a cliff. Except this guy was vertical. His claws left skid marks in the bead board. I lined up for his next attempt and wished I had something with an edge to it. The baseball bat might render some monsters senseless, but as well as thick hides, goblins also have thick skulls.

I knelt down as he took a flying leap at me and knew I needed to get down to the kitchen for some cutlery. I fired a couple bullets at him, which knocked him back but didn't do much to slow him down. In fact, it just made him come at me angrier and faster. I backed out of the room and just about tripped over Mac as he ran right behind my feet.

"Cat! Get out of here before you get me killed!" I

shouted.

Mac scrambled down the steps and I figured the cat had a good plan. I tore off behind him. I could hear the goblin gobbling up the distance between us. I grabbed ahold of the wooden banister and swung around, using my speed to boomerang myself into the kitchen. I had one of those fancy knife blocks on the counter and started throwing them at the goblin like a circus sideshow star. If I ever decided to take up a second career, turns out I had a real skill for narrowly missing a target. I grazed one of his ears, which wasn't effective at all. I grabbed my toaster oven and used it to whack him on the side of the head as I looked around for something else. I opened the refrigerator door and used it as a shield as he ran headlong towards me. My feet slid on the floor. Rolling pins, cookie sheets, I pretty much emptied my cupboards as I threw everything except the kitchen sink at him. And I seriously would have ripped the kitchen sink right out of the wall if I thought it would slow him down. Where were all of those dangers that people were always warning you to watch out for in a kitchen? I was in need of a fatal home accident. I threw him the microwave, which he caught in his two hands, and then I turned the water sprayer on full blast thinking maybe I could at least electrocute the guy. Only managed to blow a fuse.

I fired off another round to buy myself another second or two. I ran into the living room and my eyes landed on a fireplace shovel. I had a fireplace shovel. I picked it up and barely had time to turn around and smash him as he came at me. The metal cast iron worked nice. Iron and Other Siders don't mix. I used the sharp edge to drive him back, giving him a whack when he got a little too close for comfort.

I totally missed remembering I had a coffee table, though.

I stumbled as my leg bashed into it sideways and fell onto my sofa. I had just enough time to reflect for a moment how stupid I was going to feel if I got killed by a stupid goblin in my own stupid home when I managed to bring down a flippin' vampire dragon…

I rolled to the side as the goblin leaped. His claws got all tangled up in the couch he and/or his buddies ripped up earlier.

"That's why you should keep things tidy until you're sure you won't need them in the middle of a battle!" I shouted at him as his fingernails got caught in a spring. He tried to lunge at me, but the couch wasn't letting go.

In the midst of all this, my phone kept going off.

I realized I did have something in the room that would be useful. I fucking hated to have to resort to this because it meant I wasn't coming back to my house. But sometimes you gotta make some hard choices. By my fireplace, I had some lighter fluid and a box of long matches. I grabbed the bottle, sprayed it on the tangled goblin, and set that mutha on fire. I scooped up Mac, who was sitting on the kitchen counter now, just watching all of this go down, and ran out the front door.

I could hear the goblin crashing around the inside of the house and I knew he was spreading the flames everywhere he went. Oh, how I loved my house. Oh, how I hated that I had to sacrifice it in order to save my own life. But a real estate witch plucked it out of my head and built it. If I ever got money again, a real estate witch could do it again. For now, I had the two most important things: my life and my idiot cat. I squeezed Mac tightly as my phone continued to ring. I pulled it out of my pocket.

"Hey, Mom…" I said as the flames began to spread.

"Maggie! Don't set your house on fire."

"Too late. Mind if I come over for dinner?"

CHAPTER FOUR

I walked over to my car, put Mac inside, and got in. He settled on the dashboard in a patch of sun and matched the sound of my engine with his own loud, contented purr. It's good to be a cat and not be concerned about a house burning to the ground.

"We always land on our feet, don't we?" I said as I gave him a scratch behind his orange ears. He rolled over onto his back. "Feet, Mac, feet."

I drove as fast as I could to the office. The greengrocer downstairs was puttering around like no one had just been attacked by a goblin or set her home on fire. The shades in M&K Tracking were up, which meant Killian was probably stirring. Or was it someone else? My senses were on high alert and I was starting to freak out a bit. Was the building being watched? Had I been followed? Was there someone waiting for me? I parked behind the building and told myself I could do this. I tucked Mac inside my leather coat and dashed to the unobtrusive entrance located by the side of the shop. I couldn't help bounding up the stairs. I preferred to be out of the hall and safely inside the four walls of the M&K Office. It had more elbowroom to throw a punch if worse went to worse. Or pull out a bazooka.

At first glance, things seemed all right. No one lurking in the shadows. No doors hanging from their hinges. The frosted glass inset advertising our place was still intact and the gold lettering that read "M&K Tracking" looked as fresh as the day it had been painted. I couldn't help sighing sadly. It seemed like it barely had time to dry before I went and fucked things up. Typical me maneuver. I turned the black handle and pushed the door open without going inside. You know, just in case something was waiting to jump me. I'd seen enough James Bond movies.

There was someone inside. Someone who was always waiting to jump me, but not in that way. I spun into the room and closed the heavy, oak door behind me.

Killian had been taking down the plants and ivy he had cultivated to take over his side of the room. The office looked positively bare without the vines that could be hypothetically bewitched by some hypothetical disgruntled client to strangle a hypothetical investigator. I always hated those damned plants. I tried to remind myself of that as my heart was hit by an uncomfortable pang of emotion. I fucking hated emotions more than I hated those damn plants.

Killian gave me one glance, and I guess I looked shitty enough to inspire a whistle. "Everything go all right with the police?"

"I think a goblin may have eaten the police. Or the police hired a goblin to eat me," I replied, opening my jacket and taking Mac safely out. I tried lowering him gently to the floor, but he jumped down, streaked across the room, and leaped up on the windowsill to smooth his ruffled fur.

Killian turned to Mac and asked him, "Any insight into who the perpetrator might have been?"

Mac just licked his paw and started washing his ears.

Killian went back to his packing. "Did you get the goblin?"

"Yes, but I had to set my house on fire."

"That seems a little extreme."

"One does what one must." I filled up a coffee mug with water so Mac could have something to drink and set it down for him. "Besides, what's a house? Just a place to sleep and store your crap."

Killian wasn't buying it but didn't press. He knew what I wasn't saying, namely how much all this sucked. Instead, he just asked, "Where are you going to stay now?"

"I'm going to have dinner with my parents tonight and figure it out."

"That seems like an especially cruel end to the sort of day you have been having."

"Mom already yelled at me on the phone before I had a chance to ignore her call."

"Will you stay with them?"

"Maybe. Or maybe head over to Mindy's place. Or something," I replied, exhausted just from thinking about it. Why the hell had someone sent goblins over to my place?

"You know you can always sleep with me."

I gave him the side-eye.

He held up his hands. "I am not propositioning you this time, Maggie. Other times, yes. Not this time. Stay in the elfin forest with me. We can provide you with needed protection."

I wiped my face. "Let me think on it, Killian. I've got to find whatever is going to heal your Queen and I've got a feeling it isn't anywhere in the elfin forest. Trekking through those trees and rabbit trails on a daily basis would be one helluva commute."

"There is no better place for you to stay. Any invasion by the forces of darkness will be seen as an act of war."

"The elves can't afford a war right now just for some dumb human chick."

"We tend to kill most things before they reach the capitol."

"But not all," I said, reminding him of the facts. "Your people have been decimated. I can't go bringing more death and destruction your way."

"As you humans would say, 'Bring it,'" said Killian, throwing his arms open wide with an awkward angle to his fingers and wrists. Killian had been watching too many battle-of-the-dance-crew movies.

"And what would I do there?" I asked. "There's stuff I gotta do. Worlds I gotta save. I need to gather up Father Killarney, form a partnership with Xiaoming to figure out why all these World Walking guild members keep disappearing, get Lacy on our payroll officially. Heck, I need to rent a satellite office somewhere on Earth to be the operational HQ for our awesome new gang."

"You can do it all," insisted Killian. "Come with me! We shall search through my people's ancient texts to see if we can find a way to free the queen. You can still make arrangements across worlds, but from a place of safety and peace."

"Safety AND peace? That doesn't sound like me."

"And," continued Killian, "you can still work with Father Killarney. Allow him and Xiaoming to finesse the details of the Earth-side operations." He then very chivalrously offered, "And I shall, personally, invite Lacy to join our merry troupe."

I gave him a knowing smirk and folded my arms. "Guess now the queen's trapped, she can't exactly enforce her no-dating policy, huh Killian?"

"One must always draw towards the light when darkness descends," replied Killian, placing his hand over his heart and gazing beatifically at the ceiling. This action caused him to start coughing, which reminded me that my buddy wasn't exactly in fit-and-fab shape. He was having none of my pity, however. He held up his finger to stop me from saying anything. "Besides, if I am to perish, I would like to express to Lacy my true feelings of gratitude for all the assistance she has given us."

"Gratitude, huh?" I replied.

"Extreme gratitude. To reflect the multiple ways she has contorted and bent over backwards to see to our missions' satisfaction."

I laughed, which is exactly the response he was looking for. Figured if a guy was on his deathbed, a pity chuckle was the least I could provide. He had the crap beaten out of him not 48-hours ago by his queen. While there were some ambrosia nectars that could speed the healing process, the absence of her life force was like watching an entire race succumb to tuberculosis.

He reached out and took my hand between his two palms. "Come with me, Maggie."

How is a person supposed to resist an elf begging her to let him solve all her problems? Especially when the only other option was moving into her parents' garage? "No braiding daisies into my hair?" I clarified, pointing my free finger accusingly at him.

But he didn't have a chance to respond because suddenly, a swarm of police cars surrounded the building.

"What's going on…" I said, backing away from the window.

"Hide, Maggie," Killian said watching as they poured out of their cruisers and stormed onto the streets. His face was set with determination. Killian's pretty laid-back and takes most things in due course. But every now and again, someone does something to piss him off. And this was one of those times.

I wasn't going to argue. I walked over to the corner of the file cabinet and felt around the edges. There was the trusty ol' click I was looking for and the bookcase swung away, revealing a small opening in the lower part of the wall.

"You never told me that existed!" Killian exclaimed.

"You don't go into the tracking business without

sometimes needing a place to hide," I replied as I knelt, crawled inside, and shut the door behind me.

What Killian didn't know was this was actually a double blind. For everyone else, it was just a little space between the walls to hang out and listen to what was going on. But Dad and I had also built ourselves a little illegal portal that led to a small pocket in space and time. It was a bitch to get into and a bitch to get out of, but that meant that only a World Walker of our caliber would have the ability to come after us.

I held off going into the dimensional safe room for the moment, though. I wanted to hear what was going down, firsthand.

I heard a pounding at the door and Killian shout, "Coming!"

His footsteps indicated he was taking his sweet ol' time to stroll over and open it. Immediately, I heard the heavy shoes of the Other Side's finest.

"Where is she?" a voice growled.

"I can still smell her…" said another.

"I am sorry, may I be of assistance?" asked Killian amidst the sound of moving bodies and scraping furniture.

"Search the building!" barked the first voice. The stirring feet quieted as most of the folks exited into the hall.

"We have a warrant for the arrest of Margaret Gertrude Mary MacKay," the man announced.

"Of what crime is she accused?" asked Killian.

"An officer of the law was on duty at her house last night. That house was burned to the ground and the officer's body was found with considerable damage. She is wanted for murder."

"This is the Other Side," mentioned Killian. "That does not mean Maggie committed murder."

"Ms. MacKay's psychic signature was the last recorded going into the crime scene. AND we have a witness who saw the accused running from the house as flames engulfed her home… carrying a cat."

I heard Mac meow a little hello for being acknowledged. Idiot animal.

"We should place the cat into custody," remarked one of the men.

"I assure you, that is unnecessary," Killian said in a shocked tone. "This is not the cat you are looking for."

"Is this your cat?" asked the officer.

"The cat is a permanent resident of these premises," Killian lied.

"Can you provide an alibi for the cat?"

"He was sleeping in a sunbeam earlier. Prior to that, he was chasing imps. He is a cat."

"Can the grocer downstairs corroborate your story?" The man's voice shifted as if he was speaking to the man beside him. "Just in case, put 'catnapping' down on the charges until we find the cat she stole."

I heard Killian sigh. "I, as an emissary of the Elfin queen, shall of course cooperate to the fullest extent required by Other Side law." Go Killian, reminding them of his diplomatic immunity! "My partner, Margaret Gertrude Mary MacKay, was here," he continued, "but she left to get a sandwich. I imagine that with the number of cars you have parked out front to bring in one woman, she will not be returning."

I heard the other officers return. "I can still smell her," said the one.

"Please feel free to continue your search," said Killian. "There is nothing to hide here."

I wished he would stop being so gawddamned obliging about it all. I heard a crash.

"Now," warned Killian, "I am cooperating fully. Any further damage to the physical property of this location will result in an invoice for the full replacement value."

The first guy grunted. "You better not be playing us for a chump, elf."

"I can assure you that any further continuation of your

search will prove to be fruitless."

The first guy said accusingly, "You pass along to that girlfriend of yours—"

"—in the interest of preserving her honor, we are not romantically involved—"

"—that if she turns herself in, this will go a lot easier for her than if I find her."

"I will relay your message if I have contact with her," Killian replied. "Now, if you gentlemen would see yourselves out."

I waited for probably a good half hour until Killian finally said, "You can come out, Maggie. They have left someone to monitor the entrances and the exits, but it is safe for now."

The cabinet swung open and Killian was crouched down to help me out. My legs were wobbly like jelly.

"Maggie," he said, shaking his head, "you have most certainly 'pissed off' someone powerful."

CHAPTER FIVE

Utilizing a carefully choreographed stop-drop-and-roll through the dimensions, I was able to get out of the office building without being seen. It was something Dad had put together and taught to me when I joined him at work. He lined up the position of the office with Earth in such a way that if you step in exactly the right spot, you can jump through dimensions and find yourself on a cliff edge in Griffith Park. If you don't know where to step, you'll find yourself standing in Griffith Park, but just off the edge in midair. It wasn't the warmest welcome a person could extend to an uninvited guest, but that was sort of the point. Dad said if there were World Walkers with a score to settle, at least we'd have a fighting chance. Sometimes I got the feeling Dad may have owed a lot of people money before I came along for the ride.

So, I bopped over to earth, crawled down the face of the cliff, wound my way past a host of hikers who were only interested in making sure I wasn't some movie mogul who could give them a job, and then I popped back onto the Other Side. My car was parked out front but there was no reason to go moving it now. Standard procedure dictated that the police leave a tracking spell on one of the bumpers. I'd let Killian handle that mess.

Instead, I just slunk my way down the streets of the Other Side, trying to keep my head low. I would have hired a cab, but I hadn't had a chance to go to the ATM before we got raided. The fact they busted in on my work meant they were probably already looking to track me, and a large withdrawal from my account was one of the easiest ways to find a person. Fuckers.

What a lousy day.

About an hour later, I showed up on Mom and Dad's block. Mom was out in the front garden. She was wearing a big, floppy straw hat over her tight, red curls. Her gardening muumuu, a pink cotton dress featuring a smaller pattern of flowers, billowed in the breeze. She waved at me as I opened the gate and then got up, dusted off her knees, and gave me a kiss on the cheek.

"Have you contacted that fat elf yet?" she asked, pointing her trowel at me.

"What?" I asked, climbing up the concrete steps to her psychic-eye shop and propping open the metal screen door. I have no idea how she knew about Trovac and why he popped into her head as the solution to my problems.

Trovac was the head of the elfin smuggling ring. He had a coffee shop downtown, just off Skid Row, called El Diablo. I was not exactly sure whose side he was on. I had a feeling it was pretty much whoever had the largest wallet. When Dad smuggled vampire relics, Trovac was the one who told him what to go after. When I smuggled vampire relics, Trovac became my contact. But even though he hooked me up, I wouldn't say I liked the guy.

Mom followed me, shaking her head. "I was just thinking you should contact that elf your father used to work for."

She brushed past me as I protested, "Mom, I can barely take care of the elf I've got. And now you want me to go hang out with another?"

"Well, it is just something to think about."

Her Leaf It Be tearoom was bathed in the dim afternoon sun. There were poofy couches and poofy footstools littering the room.

"No," I said as I followed her in. The metal door clanged shut with what I hoped was some finality. "No, there is nothing to think about."

"What aren't you thinking about?" asked Dad from the kitchen. He peeked through the beaded curtain. His shaggy, dirty-blonde-and-gray hair was in desperate need of a haircut. He was dressed in a black t-shirt and jeans, his regular uniform for working around the house.

"Mom wants me to see Trovac."

"Listen to your mother, Maggie."

"Don't take her side."

He gave me a look like he didn't want me to listen to her at all, but she was standing right there and sometimes it is easier to pretend to agree than to argue. That I could agree with.

I turned back to Mom. "I'll consider it."

She took off her hat and placed her gardening gloves and trowel inside. She fluffed her permed hair into an orange pom-pom. "That's all I want. Really, you think I was asking you to consider something absolutely ridiculous. All I'm asking is for you to think about it."

I breathed deeply and tried to suppress the urge to say something I would regret.

"I mean, it isn't like your decision making skills are anything to be trusted," she continued.

"What?"

"You burned your house down, Maggie."

Dad stepped fully out of the kitchen, his uneaten sandwich in his hand. "You did WHAT?"

I waved him off. "There was a break-in last night. There was a goblin."

"So, you bash him over the head with a mace, Maggie. You don't burn your house down."

"All my maces were locked up because he bashed in my armory and I had to do what I had to do."

He shook his head and bit into his sandwich.

"Also," I mentioned casually, "I'm wanted for murder."

Dad started choking and Mom had to go pound him on the back.

"She was set up," she explained to him.

"Yes," I added. "Yes, it was a total setup. The goblin attacked me and I had to flee the scene because he had called for reinforcements. I don't even know if he was an actual goblin. He could have been a doppelganger."

Dad came over and poked my forehead with his forefinger. "Did you melt your brains in that fire, Maggie? Because it sounds like you aren't thinking so good. You let them take you. You let Lacy spring you. And everything works out just fine and no one has to go burning down any houses."

"Dad…" I explained, "The World Walkers would have used that medusa we hauled in to turn me into a statue if I had let them take me. THAT is why I burned down my house."

"Well, why didn't you say so," he replied, taking another bite of his sandwich.

"I think I need to get out of town until things cool down."

"Well, at least let me pack you something for the journey," said Mom, strolling into the kitchen like putting together a sack dinner for a fugitive daughter was what we did every Sunday night.

"Why?" asked Dad. "Stay here. We'll put out the sofa bed."

As appealing as the thought sounded, sleeping on a sofa bed in the tea shop while he and Mom made midnight runs to the refrigerator, I declined. "So, the elfin queen is dying," I explained. "Killian and I have to close up shop while he tries to save his people from the inside and I try to figure out how to save his people from the outside."

"What?" asked Dad, clarifying he had heard what he thought he heard.

I didn't want to go into it. I just waved his question away like it was something I had under control. Which I didn't. But he didn't need to know that.

"Jesus, Maggie..." he replied. He put his hands on his waist and shook his head in disappointment. "You don't do things by half, do you? She's dying?"

"It might be my fault."

He walked away, completely giving up on me.

"Thanks for setting up the back exit in the office, by the way," I offered, trying to put a positive spin on things. "Ended up being really useful to have some dimensions to jump through."

"You're welcome...? MAGGIE! You don't go around killing the queen of the elves!!"

"If Killian's busy, can you pick up the car and take care of the office?"

"Where's your car??"

"Well, when the office was raided, I had to make a run for it."

"THE OFFICE WAS RAIDED?!"

"I'm hoping Killian will bring it over before the parking tickets rack up."

"And how, exactly, were you planning on getting out of Dodge?" he asked as if this was the biggest issue facing my life right now.

I sat down on one of Mom's big armchairs and almost disappeared into the cushion. "Can I borrow your car?" I asked.

"Trovac has so many connections..." Mom called out from the kitchen.

"I'M NOT CALLING TROVAC!"

"Really, Maggie," she huffed with exasperation. "I am just trying to help." I heard her leave the kitchen and go into the dining room.

Dad shook his head and came to sit next to me. He

offered me half his sandwich and I took it. "Well, you know you're on to something if you've got this many people after you," he pointed out. I think he meant it as encouragement.

"I would have settled for a participation ribbon."

He patted my knee as he chewed. "Well, what's YOUR plan? The one that doesn't involve Trovac."

I sighed heavily. "Okay, Killian said I can hide out in the elfin forest for as long as I need. Maybe I just need to keep my head low until the heat from all this passes over."

"Great plan. Just hide until everyone is dead. But come out when it is safe for you! That DEFINITELY sounds like a well-thought-out strategy, Maggie."

"That's not MY plan," I pointed out. "That's Killian's plan."

"Fucking elves."

"Hey, he means well," I replied, sticking up for my partner who was offering me a whole heck of a lot more than a pull-out couch.

"He'll be braiding flowers in your hair within two weeks."

"Take that back."

"One week."

"I already made him promise no flowers."

"Elves lie."

I stopped him before this devolved into a discussion of my choice in business partners. "So, what would you do, huh? Just go after the vampires and the relics and hope for the best? I think that's what got me into this mess."

"You're the one who wanted to turn smuggler."

Dad, back before he got stuck in the boundary, got tangled up in a vampire relic smuggling ring. I started to get tangled up in it, too, except it turned out I had a bad sense of what was a good idea to bring across and what was a bad idea to bring across. What can I say. My gift lay in tracking down monsters, not objects.

"You said," I said, pointing out the unhelpful facts,

"that almost all World Walkers do, at one point or another."

Dad shrugged. "This isn't the first time a thing like this has happened."

"Really? Gone around killing queens yourself from time to time?"

"No," he replied. Dad poured himself a cup of tea from Mom's cooling pot. She was going to have a fit.

"Don't drink from my teapot!" Mom called from the backroom. "It clouds my vision!"

"I'm not, honey!" Dad shouted back as he totally took a sip and then set down his cup. "We did a real disservice to ourselves, here on the Other Side, that the only keepers of any sort of history are the elves and the dwarves. Look how far they've gotten in their evolution. The rest of us are limping along, just trying not to get eaten in a world that is controlled by whoever has the biggest teeth."

"Every heard of the Bringers of Light?"

"Nope. But I have a feeling you'll figure it out for us." He ruffled my hair. "Just keep your head low and the people around you few, Maggie-girl. Remember it's harder to hit a small target. And don't burn down any more buildings, okay?"

That's the thing with my family. You can go around practically destroying the multiverse, but after you talk it out, it's all good.

"So, what do you think these Light people want?" I asked. "I mean, other than to destroy the elves and rip a permanent portal to the Dark Dimension." I ticked off all the things I knew about this group. "One nutcase group to rule them all?" I offered.

Dad shrugged. "I don't know, Maggie-girl. The schemes and struggles of the social climbers are ones I will never understand."

"Well, speaking of climbing," I said, hauling myself out of the chair. "I need to climb out of this dimension and find a hideout with rent that runs on the cheap side."

"I'll keep an open ear."

"And I'll need to find some artifact or spell or something to save the queen of the elves."

"Will also spread the word amongst those I know."

"Hopefully once I get her free, she'll sort the rest of this mess out."

"That's a lot of expectation to place on one person, Maggie," Dad cautioned.

"Figure if anyone can bring these bastards to heel, she's the bitch to do it."

"Maggie," Dad admonished.

"Have you met the woman? She's not winning any prizes for congeniality."

Dad got a faraway look in his eye. He took another sip of Mom's all-seeing tea. If I didn't know better I'd have said he was channeling her a bit. "Your mom might be right…"

"What?" I asked, aiming towards the door so we could be out of the house before Mom discovered she was going to have to steep a few more leaves.

"You should let me call Trovac," Dad replied. He took a swallow and then put his cup down without using a coaster, which meant Mom was going to have an even bigger fit inside all the other fits she was already having.

"Okay," I replied, this time, ushering him in the garage-direction with my flailing arms like some sort of stewardess in the middle of an emergency evacuation.

Dad stood up and brushed the crumbs from his jeans. "Give me a few minutes to make some calls, Maggie-girl."

CHAPTER SIX

"So you need me to smuggle your daughter across the border?" Trovac said through the receiver.

"I wouldn't call if it wasn't an emergency," my dad explained.

We were sitting in the kitchen with the family's goldenrod-colored phone receiver between us. Dad had installed a little booster to the earpiece so it sort of worked like a conference phone if everyone else in the house stayed absolutely silent. It was one of those infomercial rip-offs that, when it was all said and done, ended up costing more than a new phone.

"Emergencies mean trouble." I could hear Trovac chewing on his gross, wet cigar as he responded. "I thought that sneaking people across the boundary is what you people did. Who do you expect me to call when the people who I hire to smuggle people aren't capable of smuggling people?"

"Listen, this problem involves your people and your queen..."

"Do not bring that into this conversation," replied Trovac, his hackles all up. Someone was feeling the effects of the queen's drain and, boy, was he cranky.

"We can get Maggie to Earth," reassured my dad. "We can pop over anyplace we feel like. But once Maggie's there, I need someone to pick her up and hide her."

"That's a liability for me," said Trovac. "I don't like taking on liabilities."

"I did a ton of jobs for you," my dad reminded him, "I risked my life many times."

"And you got paid."

"Yes, I got paid."

"Are you paying me for this?"

Dad gave a huge sigh and looked at me. Right now, they were living off Mom's psychic-eye shop income and the pittance Dad had set aside for retirement. They didn't have the sort of funds to front me the money.

I swallowed hard. "I could owe you a favor," I said.

That made Trovac stop. Dad gave me a warning look and shook his head. It was a couple seconds before Trovac's voice popped back on the phone. "A favor, huh?"

Favors were binding contracts between a human and the fae, and favors were never called in because someone had a pleasant task they needed done. They were messy and costly and I probably would be safer letting the Bringers of Light haul me in.

Suddenly, my cell phone buzzed notifying me I had a text. It was a message from Lacy, our blue girl over at prison intake. It read: "Graham busted out."

I leaned into the phone. "Whatever you want. I bind myself to you. Set me up and keep me safely hidden on Earth and I, Maggie MacKay, will owe you one favor."

"You have yourself a deal," said Trovac. "I'll be in touch with the location in ten minutes."

And then there was a click and the line went dead.

"What happened, Maggie?" my dad asked as he unscrewed the detachable speaker and rescrewed the normal earpiece onto the phone.

Graham is the second-best bounty hunter on the Other Side, aside from me. Back in the good old days, he'd pick up my leftovers

He also technically is classified as an "angel." That means he is able to fly instead of walk, which happens to make tracking the guy or guessing where he is coming from a real pain in the ass. Oh, and before you get too wrapped up in the angel thing, "angel" is just a term for people with wings. In other dimensions, humans evolved to fly. When some of those fluttering idiots broke through the boundary to Earth, the folks on Earth were so gob smacked, they labeled them as "angels." But angels are just assholes like you and me. I'd put cash money down on a bet that some con artist in the flock was able to convince a Bronze Aged human that he was the mouthpiece of the gods. You know what they say, repeat a lie long enough and folks start thinking it's the truth...

And Graham was the biggest con artist I had met in a long time.

So, Graham was originally hired to haul me in when my permit got pulled and I refused to take advantage of the World Walker's involuntary leave program. He was also the one who tricked me into bringing over the stone that trapped the queen. Then he opened the portal to the Dark Dimension with it. The guy's a genuine, all-around jerk.

But, let the record show, I was the one who hauled him in.

Of course, that meant he was probably on his way to haul me in to somewhere very unpleasant this very moment.

I showed him the text. "Lacy says Graham broke out of prison."

Dad sprang from his chair. "Get in the car, Maggie. We're going now."

Yeah, it was that bad.

"Bye, Mom!" I called out.

She wandered in with a Tupperware full of dinner. "I

knew you wouldn't be able to stay. You're never able to stay."

I gave her a kiss on the cheek. "I promise to stay sometime when I'm not on the run."

"I'll hold you to it. You should go now," she said. I wasn't sure if that was her mom voice or her psychic voice talking, but either/or, it seemed like good advice. She then shoved a wad of bills in my hand. "Just until you get your bank account set up. Your father will come over as soon as he can."

"Thanks," I said. "You're taking all this so much better than I would have expected."

"Oh, Maggie," she replied, pushing back my hair. "It all turns out just fine in the end. But only if you leave now. Otherwise, we're all going to die horribly. So you should go."

Well, that settled that.

Dad was already in the garage and I ran out into the night. Times like these I hated that the garage was not attached to the house and the walkway was open for all the world to see. I scanned the skies for Graham.

Unfortunately, it wasn't Graham, but another flying jerk that was keeping an eye on me.

"DAD!" I shouted as I booked it towards the garage door.

He poked his head out the side.

"We have vampires."

"Damnnit, Maggie," he said, disappearing back into the garage.

I pulled out my stake and ran. The vampires couldn't enter the yard. The family perimeter was strong and we were safe in our cocoon of MacKay safety. But the moment we left the garage, we were fair game.

I got inside and slammed the door behind me. Not that the thin, wooden walls of the garage made us any more safe than before, I just fundamentally felt a little safer when there was a door between me and the bad guys.

"Come out! Come out, Maggie MacKay!" hissed a voice circling outside.

Dad was in his toolbox, scrounging around for his spare stakes. "You're graduating head of the class in 'ruining your father's night', Maggie."

"I didn't mean for any of this," I pointed out as he loaded up his tool belt with all sorts of pointy things.

"You never do, Maggie."

"Don't act like this is my fault!"

"You HAD to go stumbling into a vast conspiracy, Maggie!"

"You're acting like I was looking for it!"

"Well, it just seems like you have an awful lot of luck tracking it down."

"You're getting to sound a lot like Mom."

"Maybe you should switch from saying you track down monsters to you track down trouble."

"It comes looking for me!"

"We will discuss this AFTER we take down that vampire," he said, loading up weapons onto the bench seat of his 1967 powder blue Ford Galaxie. Modern cars with their fancy computers tend to short out when jumping through portals.

I opened the door. "Fine."

"Fine."

Dad got in and slammed his door.

"Seatbelt," I reminded him.

He barely was able to keep the words he was muttering under his breath from becoming words he was just muttering. He hit the clicker, peeled out of the garage, and then hit the clicker again to close the door behind us. We weren't even halfway down the block when the vampire landed on the roof.

I pulled out my gun.

"DON'T put holes in my ceiling, Maggie," he said, grabbing my forearm.

I couldn't believe him. "There is a vampire on our

roof. Don't you think you can pony up for a little body repair?"

"Maggie, we seriously need to work on the fine art of finesse."

"Everything I learned, I learned from you!" I pointed out.

"Don't throw that at me. I did not teach you to go shooting holes in a perfectly good roof that doesn't belong to you. Those are some bad habits you picked up on your own."

"Well, if you hadn't gotten yourself trapped in the boundary for two years, maybe I wouldn't have had to figure all this out on my own."

"I did it to protect you!"

I heard the thumping on the roof. "He's going to punch his nails through the roof any minute now."

"Not if I can help it," said Dad, cornering the car hard.

As the vampire struggled to stay on, the nails came through the roof.

"Can I shoot him now?" I asked.

"No, Maggie. No, you may not. You're already wanted for murder and I'm not leaving behind a vampire corpse riddled with bullets from any one of your guns."

"He is going to open up your roof like a tin can if you don't handle this now," I warned him.

Dad slammed on the brakes and the vampire went flying out into the street. "Fine, Maggie. Fine. Since you seem to have it all worked out how I, a person twice your age who has been doing this since before you were born, should handle this, why don't you show me how you see fit."

"FINE! I will!" I opened the door and then slammed it behind me, palming my stake in my hand. "WHAT is your ISSUE, vampire?! Can't you see my Dad and I are having a REALLY bad day."

"Maggie MacKay, you are the one with a bounty on her head…"

"Blah blah blah. Vaclav or Bringers of Light?"

The vampire looked at me as if he was startled. "How did you know…?"

"Which one? If I'm going to get killed by a stupid vampire, I want to know who hired him."

"The Briiiingers of the Liiiiiight…" he hissed.

"Thank you," I said. And then I winged my stake at him and it struck him square in the heart. He looked down at it in confusion before falling to his knees and dying. I mean, dying again. He was already dead.

I walked over, placed my Doc Marten on his chest and yanked out my silver stake. I wiped off the vampire slime onto the grass and walked back to the car.

"Well?" asked Dad.

"The Bringers of Light are after me."

"And you wanted to shoot him through the roof," Dad grumbled.

"Yeah, yeah…" I grumbled back, resting my elbow on the windowsill.

"You can't just go around shooting things, Maggie."

"Since when?"

"Since right now."

"Whatever."

We drove the rest of the way in silence.

Family.

CHAPTER SEVEN

We arrived at the appointed spot. It was a more remote location in the Other Side. If we had continued down the road, we would have hit Ghost Town, although Ghost Town wasn't technically a ghost town anymore since Mom crossed all of them over. It was just an empty village falling apart in the middle of the desert.

Dad got out and waited as I gathered up Mom's Tupperware filled with lasagna. He rested against the hood of the car with his arms folded. "Promise me you'll be careful."

I patted my jacket pocket to make sure I had my wallet, then pulled out my keys and handed them over. "Killian's cleaning the office out," I explained. "If you could just keep an eye on things. Collect rent from the greengrocer downstairs."

"Nice you have an income property to keep you afloat," he said.

"Yep," I replied. "I'll give you a call as soon as I get settled."

"Don't," he said.

"What?"

"They'll trace the call, Maggie-girl."

I pulled the cell phone out of my pocket and handed that over, too. Guess that's why my dad managed to keep what he did under wraps for so long.

He took out the battery and smashed the phone on the ground. "Trovac will figure out a way for people to get ahold of you. I know you'll show up when things are safe. And if things aren't safe, I'm pretty sure your mother will know how to find you before anyone else does."

I nodded. We stood there for a moment, staring up at the night sky together. "Thanks. Thanks for helping me through this."

"That's what dads are for," he said, giving me a great big bear hug and then cuffing me on the side of the head. "Now get over there and find out what hell you signed up for, giving a favor to that elf. Idiot."

I stepped away and turned. I reached out my hand. The boundary was soft and mushy at this point in the veil. I gave one final look back and smile, and thought maybe I caught a glint of something wet on my dad's cheek, then I pushed through.

I ended up behind a gas station in the middle of nowhere. It was brandless. Nothing but a hand-painted green-on-white sign that read "Gas" over the door. There were two sad, lonely pumps and some clunkers parked next to a rundown garage and a stack of old tires. A sign in the window said, "No Public Restrooms." It was the kind of place a person only stops when desperate. Desperate to be murdered.

About half-a-mile away, I could see headlights zooming down a long, lonely stretch of highway. The night air was filled with the sounds of desert insects, which, let me tell you, are a hell of a lot better than Other Side insects, but otherwise the atmosphere was just about as flipping creepy.

I opened the door to the convenience store and walked inside. A bell tinkled overhead. There were a couple of working florescent lights, but also one that was buzzing loudly and another that kept flickering on and off. The guy behind the counter was staring blankly at a soccer game on a small television set. From the skunk-like smell of the room, I had a couple ideas why expending the energy to change the overhead lightbulb seemed like just too much.

I cleared my throat and got no reaction from him. I cleared it again, this time a little louder and with more insistence. He looked at me, his jaw hanging slack.

"I'm here to see a guy about an elf...?"

He blinked slowly, then pulled out a set of keys and an envelope from below the counter and handed them to me. "There's a car out there for you."

"Where?" I asked, glancing outside the window.

He pointed to the row of rusty vehicles, all circa nondescript 1980. Then it seemed like even pointing took too much energy.

"Thanks," I said. "Live each day to the fullest, my friend."

He went back to watching his game.

I opened the envelope and there was a wad of cash. I read a little note that basically explained, in not so many words, that I couldn't pull anything out of an ATM while I was walking on the bad side of the law. In exchange for a wire transfer my family would need to make to the elf, including a transaction fee that bordered on extortion, he'd provide me with an all-cash weekly allowance. I glanced around the convenience store to see if there was anything I was going to need for the night, and then figured I'd figure it out later. The clerk was in no condition to do math.

I walked out and clicked the fob to try to figure out which pile of metal was going to be my trusty steed. The lights on a beater of a brown car flashed on. That fat elf had more money than any fae creature had any business having and he gave me a POS car.

I climbed inside. The smell of orange car fresheners

battled it out with my mom's lasagna. I poured the rest of the envelope's contents onto the stained passenger seat. There was a cell phone as well as a paper map. There was a note on the phone: "For Emergencies Only." Guess I wasn't going to be using GPS for this trip. Here's to kicking it old skool.

I turned out of the gas station and hated the fact there was not a single street lamp anywhere around this godforsaken part of the world. I kept driving, following the directions on the piece of paper until I turned into a grody looking neighborhood. I guess that's why I got the shitty car. Camouflage. There were cars of a similar vintage parked up and down the sidewalks. And set up on blocks sans tires. The houses had more furniture on the lawns than they had inside. I finally turned into a cul-de-sac and found a small, ramshackled bungalow that matched the address I was given. It was covered in crumbling, brown stucco and the property was bordered by a wall of decorative cinder blocks. The yard was dead. There was a bleached out Little Tykes plastic car sitting next to a leafless tree. It had a garage, though. I pressed the clicker on the visor and it opened. The inside of the garage was stuffed with old paint cans and boxes. There was just enough room for me to pull the car inside.

I got out, opened the door leading to the house, and sighed.

It was clean, but old. The carpet was the color of dirt and had a pattern sculpted into its weave. The lights overhead were yellow and barely illuminated the place. There was a single, full-sized bed in an empty bedroom, with one pillow and a sleeping bag. The kitchen featured a few plastic plates and cups someone must have picked up at the 99-cent store. The dining room featured a card table and some rickety chairs. I rested my hands on my waist and sighed again.

Home sweet home.

45

CHAPTER EIGHT

I slept restlessly. What can I say. You've get a bunch of bad guys gunning for you, plus a new bed, and sleep just doesn't come the way you want it. I was up with the sun and rarin' to get a gander at the new neighborhood before the pink left the sky.

I opened the closet and saw that Trovac had left me some clothes. Mom-slacks in the world's most bland shade of beige and a solid powder-blue t-shirt that didn't even deserve description. I put them on and looked at myself in the mirror. Très PTA meeting chic. If there is one thing the elf got right, it was about disappearing in plain sight.

I peered out the window. No one came out of any of the houses for work. No one wandered down the street. I didn't even see a curtain move. The neighborhood was so flippin' deserted, I would have guessed the Rapture had happened if I didn't know the Four Horsemen were locked up in an Other Side prison after a particularly nasty all-night bender through the Middle East. Some cowboys just don't know how to hold their liquor. I let the blind fall back into place. I guess the elf had moved me into a neighborhood of agoraphobics, which worked for me.

I climbed into the car, opened the garage, and drove out. I was so far away from a town, the city didn't bother with sweeping the street or mowing the median. It was covered in stunted, weedy grass. I literally had no idea where I was, but I had a feeling that was the point. You can't accidentally blow your cover and let it slip where you are if you don't know where "where you are" is.

I finally came to what seemed like some semblance of civilization. All of the shops had hand-painted signs in Spanish, but nothing was open. There wasn't a chain store for as far as my eyes could see. I was a tracker and probably could have used my voodoo powers to find a Target, but I didn't know how advanced the bad guys' trackers might be. I didn't need to go leaving psychic signatures in places where there were no other psychic signatures to cover it up.

I eventually pulled in front of a little mom 'n pop grocery/liquor store and walked in. There was a short, potbellied man behind the counter. He was wearing a trucker hat and a plaid flannel shirt, and not ironically.

"Hey!" I said.

He turned his watery eyes to look at me and replied, "Hey." And then he went back to staring at the television screen.

Now, one guy barely noticing my existence, and I would have attributed it to the recent legalization of certain recreational substances in the great state of California for medicinal purposes. But two guys in fewer than 12 hours made me wonder if this was a part of the elf's "Disappearance Services", too. No way a guy would be that out of it so early in the morning. There is this spell called "distraction" that doesn't render you invisible. It just renders you so boring that no one can be bothered to store you in their long-term memory bank.

I was going to owe Trovac big time.

I grabbed some bottled water and some random

breakfasty crap to gnaw on in the car while I found the town's official grocery store. I got the same treatment there. I started to think I should just save myself the hassle of paying because no one seemed to notice or care, but that's what we call a test of one's true moral fiber and I was a fugitive, not a thief. I mean, unless someone was paying me. But not on my own dime.

By the time I got back to the house, a couple hours had passed. I clicked open the garage door and entered the house with my arms filled with groceries.

"GODDAMMNIT!" I shouted, dropping my bags.

Trovac had spread out across the La-Z-Boy recliner in the living room.

"How the hell did you get in?" I grumbled as I picked up my spilled groceries and went into the kitchen.

"I own this neighborhood," said the elf. "I can 'get' into whatever house I feel like."

"Ah," I replied. "That explains the warmth and friendliness of all the neighbors I haven't met yet."

"Neighbors tend to stick their nose where it does not belong," said Trovac. "I hazarded a guess that you would appreciate an opportunity for a little silent reflection."

I sighed as I put the milk into the refrigerator. As creepy as it all was, I owed the guy my life and appreciated that he was taking it seriously. "Thanks," I said. I grabbed an orange juice out of the refrigerator. "Can I pour you a drink?"

"I am on duty," he replied.

I shrugged and put it away, but grabbed a beer for me. I don't care how early it was, I was pretty sure I was going to need a drink for whatever brought Trovac into my living room.

He had claimed the only comfortable chair in the place and I wrestled for a minute between the folding chairs and the floor. The chairs won. I didn't even want to think how many people had bled on that brown carpet. I sat down and kicked my feet up onto the other chair.

"So," I said. "Any thought on how you'd like to use that favor?"

"I have," he replied, giving me a smile that struck cold fear into the pit of my stomach. "I would like to engage you to stop the collapse of the border between Earth and the Other Side."

I breathed deep. "Well aren't we lucky? There is nothing I would rather do."

The elf smiled again, but it still held a chill. He picked up a roll of paper from beside his chair and threw it towards me. I caught it and put in on the table. It was made of vellum and felt very old.

"I will be moving you tonight to a new location," he said.

I motioned to the room. "As schwanky as these digs are, I gotta say, I'm not going to be heartbroken about pulling up stakes."

"I'm moving you to the Valley."

"Oh, hell… leave me here," I groaned.

"There are… strange things… going on."

"What sort of strange things?" I asked.

"I do not wish to color your powers of observation."

"That is a bullshit response."

He paused for a moment, as if he was collecting his thoughts. "I have reason to believe that Firebrand Studios is stealing people's negative emotions and they are feeding off this unhappiness."

"What?" I asked, making sure I was hearing things correctly. "Firebrand Studios? The most beloved of all the studios in all the world? The one that makes all the family-friendly crap on TV? They one known for their adventures-with-puppies-and-kittens movies?"

"That would be the one."

"The ENTIRE studio? I mean…" I sat forward. "Okay, there are creatures who have been known to go sucking on emotions, but an entire studio?"

He held up his hands helplessly. "I do not know if this

is caused by a person or by an object. But it is happening. That is why I need your help. I have sensed a great gathering of power and a weakness in the veil at the center of their studio lot."

"When did this all start?" I asked, looking around for a pen and paper to take notes and then remembering I didn't have a pen or a paper. I went to pull out my cell phone to send myself a text about it, but then remembered I didn't have that, either. I was going to have to resort to just listening. Like it was friggin' 1993.

Trovac didn't seem to notice, though. He was busy waxing away as elves are wont to do. "This evil seems to be centered around a group of six old, white men called The Shareholders."

"Old, white shareholders are the root of this evil?" I replied. "Tell me something the world doesn't already know."

He continued. "These Shareholders purchased Firebrand Studios in a takeover that went entirely too smoothly for a business acquisition this size."

"The Shareholders?" I repeated, still hung up on this group. "Do these guys have actual names or do they just drive around cloaked in secrecy in their evil Rolls Royces with The Shareholders written on their vanity plates?"

"So you have seen their modes of transportation?" Trovac said, looking relieved that he wasn't going to have to explain everything to me.

"No, I have not!" I answered back. "Are you kidding me? 'The Shareholders' is… like… their gang name?"

"The rich and powerful are more dangerous than any street organization I have encountered, Maggie," said Trovac, pulling a cigar out of his front pocket. "Absolute power corrupts absolutely."

"Not a single name?" I clarified.

"Names have power."

This was Magic 101: true names hold power, and if you utter them, you can exert control over the subject. It's why my parents gave me such a long name with multiple spelling choices. Just the slightest twist of the tongue or missed name in the midst of things will throw the power off. I also had a couple MORE middle names that they happened to fail to put on my birth certificate, just for safekeeping.

"It is how they hide themselves in plain sight, Maggie," said Trovac, "Although you know one of the members."

"I do?"

"A certain politician who dated a certain Medusa that your father and you hauled in last year." There was just the slightest hint of accusation in his voice, like if my dad and I hadn't been so hell-bent on covering rent, this whole apocalypse thing could have been avoided.

"IT WAS JUST A JOB!" I pointed out. "We were just trying to pay our bills!"

"There is nothing more evil than a politician, Maggie," Trovac mansplained to me. "Of course, he is not a politician here on Earth. He is just another regular investor who happens to have a remarkable ability to say nothing and yet convince people to do exactly what he wants them to do."

"So, we're doomed."

"Oh, it gets worse, Maggie," said the elf leaning forward. "They kept the original CEO in power, but there have been several times he has appeared in a news conference and there is a decidedly golden glow to his eyes."

"Gold?" I repeated just to make sure I heard him right. "He had a gold eye shine?"

"Gold."

"You're telling me they replaced the CEO of the largest entertainment studio in the world with a doppelganger?"

"That is exactly what I am telling you. And I have a feeling when you step onto the lot, you'll find there are quite a few more."

"I'm going on the lot," I laughed. "Right. Me. As

what? One of People Magazine's Prettiest People of the Year winners?"

"We are going to keep your profile a bit lower," he replied.

"Good. Because I would hate to have to unseat George Clooney," I replied.

"No one can unseat George Clooney."

"Ain't that the truth."

"He is an elf, you know."

"WHAT?!"

"Impossibly attractive to humans? Endless charisma and, dare I say, glamour?"

"You fucking elves are taking over everything, aren't you," I replied.

"Well, if the Mother Tree dies, that will not be a concern anymore, will it." He lifted his sleeve and showed me his arms. It looked like there was spilled ink all over his skin, following the lines of his veins. "The life of the Mother Tree sings in our souls. As she dies, so do we. Our blood has already begun to rot."

I remembered the way that Killian had cried out when I saved him from the elfin prison and he accidentally touched the black sludge working its way through the tree. I thought of him coughing and realized his lungs were being fed with this black slime, how his heart was being fed with this decaying tar.

"It is happening to all elfin kind, even the ones who have set up their homes here on Earth. Doctors will announce some flesh eating virus or Ebola outbreak, but the rot is global and we shall all die."

I reached out to touch his arm, but stopped myself. "How much time do you have?"

"I do not know."

"I am really, really sorry about bringing that rock over to the Other Side," I offered lamely.

He waved me away as he rolled his sleeve back down. "You will find a solution or you will not. When you have lived as long as us, you realize there are worse things than dying."

"Like… having the entire world end and Earth turned into an annex of the Dark Dimension?"

"If you fail, I am glad I will not be there to see it," he replied, buttoning his cuff. "Now, as to your task."

"I'm all ears," I replied and then awkwardly apologized, realizing what he might have thought I was saying. "That was not some sideways dig at your ears or the ears of your people or the fact your ears have been surgically altered to look like human ears. And I apologize if it came across that way."

"It had not even entered my mind until you put it in there, Ms. MacKay. Thank you, for that."

"It's what I do," I replied. "Take a perfectly normal, decent conversation and make it awkward."

"Try to keep your mouth shut during this job," Trovac replied, shifting in his seat. "A more pressing issue than our blood rotting in our veins is that the power now gathering at Firebrand Studios is such that it may render the Mother Tree issue moot. As such, I have secured a position for you as a production assistant."

Oh, this elf was using this favor to put me through hell. "That is just mean."

"I assure you, it is necessary."

"You couldn't set me up as some sort of movie mogul?"

"The Firebrand Studio lot is the most secure location in all of Hollywood, but it is filled with new faces that come and go and no one in the industry will pay any attention to a woman over thirty in those clothes," he said, motioning to my mom-slacks. "No one notices the PAs."

"Touché," I replied, dryly.

He shrugged. "Do not try to fight the machine, Maggie." He looked at me with some consideration. "You will need to go without your neckguard, though."

My hand instinctively went to my throat. "Are you

kidding me?" I asked. "I've got both vampires and a secret doppelganger organization gunning for me and you want me to walk around with my carotid artery on display for all fangs to see?"

"It will make you stand out at the studio," said the elf, with just a flicker of sympathy. He reached into a paper bag beside his chair and tossed me a bottle of makeup. "Cover up the scars and move through the world like the rest of us."

Makeup doesn't cover vampire scars. Nothing covers vampire scars. I put the bottle onto the table. "Can I keep it on at least until I get to the new place?" I asked, my voice sounding a bit too much like a petulant teenager in relation to the seriousness of what he was asking of me.

"Anyone monitoring the red light cameras will see it and know it is you."

I gulped down a huge draught of the beer. My neckguard was my security blanket. I hadn't got without it since that day that one vampire tried to turn me. Every time I took it off, something happened to remind me to never leave home without it.

But the elf swore I was under his protection, so I found my hands going up to the lock and giving it a spin. What the elf didn't know was that while I might not be allowed to wear it with the work uniform and might not be able to wear it in the car, sure as shooting, it was staying with me at all times and if I could put it on, I was doing so.

Trovac's eyes got wide when he saw the scars on my neck. "You're lucky to have survived."

"I'm a stubborn old cuss," I replied, challenging him to say one word more on the matter. He kept his mouth shut, which was good for both of us. I had tucked the whole ugly affair into my repressed memories and that was exactly where I wanted it to stay.

"I shall secure you a turtleneck blouse."

I put the neckguard heavily on the table. "So, what exactly do you need me to do while I'm stuck in this vortex of suck? Besides commit heinous crimes against fashion?"

"Perhaps a scarf would be better."

"It is August."

"Scarves are quite the rage."

"Let me assure you, rage is pretty close to what I'm bordering on."

"So dramatic, Maggie," he replied, picking his teeth with his pinkie nail. "Find out who or what is gathering this power at the studio and stop it. In exchange for this, I shall provide you with my protection."

"And then we're even steven?" I said, reaching out my palm to shake on it.

"One favor in exchange for my protection," said the elf, grasping my hand in his. "That was the deal. And so, Margaret Gertrude Mary MacKay, I hereby call in the favor and bind you to the task of stopping this force that is gathering energy at the studio and weakening the veil."

I took a deep gulp of air. It had been pronounced. It was done. I had to do it. There was no other way out. Here's the thing with favors. Once it is pronounced, you gotta do what the person says they want you to do or you slowly begin to die. As soon as you accomplish it, you're restored to full health. But until then, my life was on a countdown clock.

There are many ways to die, but death in the San Fernando Valley was not the way I wanted to go.

"You got yourself a deal."

CHAPTER NINE

I watched as Trovac drove away through the creased, metal mini-blinds and then let the slats clatter closed. Fortunately, I didn't have anything to pack aside from the super glamorous stylin's hanging in my closet, and I'm pretty sure humanity would consider it a blessing from on high if I left the Fall Abomination Collection behind. Oh, I also needed to remember the Tupperware my mom sent the lasagna in to return it to her. In fact, if I were shot or stabbed or burned alive, I probably needed to make sure my corpse was found clutching the freshly cleaned plastic container as if I had been on my way to return it.

I rolled open the scroll Trovac gave me and saw he had calligraphed a very nice set of driving instructions. He also left me a wad of keys which, I hoped, would unlock the door to my new and moderately less-murdery digs. There was an ID for the Firebrand Studios movie lot, but the ID said my name was: "Molly Mackie." Close enough.

I had been so out of it, what with trying to survive and save the multiverse, I had completely missed the Firebrand merger... hostile takeover... possession... whatever Wall Street calls it when you sell your company's soul.

Firebrand Studios had their fat, cotton candy covered fingers in every corner of the film, television, music, theme park, travel, and merchandise business. The one thing that had happened to fall on even my hopelessly clueless ears was that Firebrand was closing down some beloved rides at their flagship park in SoCal and "upgrading" them to reflect some of their upcoming franchises, a move that was causing the purists to almost storm the gates with torches and pitchforks. If the Shareholders were eating negative energy, I was going to have to lift them out of their boardroom with a crane.

I loaded up the car and stuck all my new groceries in the trunk. Figured if I was living on a P.A. salary for the foreseeable future, I didn't have a lot of room to go junking the junk food.

I put my neckguard in the glove compartment and it took me a couple minutes before I could work up the courage to pull the car out of the garage. I told myself sitting there wasn't going to make anything easier, though. My best bet was to get to Los Angeles and into a threshold before dark. It was even worth getting stuck in the middle of rush hour traffic to do it. But man, there are just some things that happen in your life that are just a bitch to shake.

Once I got back onto the main road, I realized the hopping point I used to get to Earth from the Other Side was halfway to Vegas. I tried to cheer myself up as I stared at the endless taillights of the two-lane highway through the desert. The hassle I was having was the same hassle for anyone trying to find me. Shoot, if I was hunting me? I'd say forget it until Tuesday around 10:00AM. Ain't no skip worth Sunday Vegas traffic on the I-15.

One never thinks they're actually going to look forward to the smog and traffic of the LA Basin, but I greeted the yellow haze of the city like the favorite cousin bringing beer to the family reunion.

And speaking of family reunions, the freeway went right past the exit I usually took to go see my sister, Mindy. I gave it a little wave. It sucked that I shouldn't go see her until all this shit got settled. No need to go bringing this particular hell to her doorstep, especially when she was getting ready to give birth to her first baby. As my dad used to say, it's important not to treat a blister with bomb. I'm pretty sure if the forces of evil tangled with Mindy in her current condition, she would have nuked the Bringers of Light into the psychic version of a glass parking lot. And she's not even supposed to have any of Mom's powers.

I kept going until I hit Burbank, this random little corner of the San Fernando Valley. It has almost all the major freeways running through it, but you can't actually transfer from one freeway to another without getting off the highway and going through side streets and neighborhoods. It makes absolutely no sense. I have this theory the street planners actually constructed a series of permanent portals leading humanity around a dimensional sinkhole, but I haven't had a chance to test it. Yet. I was going to have plenty of time now.

I pulled off and winded around some of the backstreets near the Burbank airport. I rechecked the scroll and confirmed this was the spot. I double-checked, just to make sure. I pulled the car into the parking lot of my new apartment complex and peered up through the windshield at my new home-away-from-home. "Oh, you fucking elf," I muttered under my breath.

It was a place called the Starlike Apartments and was definitely for a clientele that was star-like, but would never quite ascend to higher heights. Have I mentioned that San Fernando is the porn capitol of the world? Yeah.

The complex looked like it was built during the "high quality" construction phase of the mid-70s and hadn't been upgraded since. At least it had some crappy looking wall A/C units poking out beneath each window. The Valley is always ten degrees different from what you find across the Hollywood Hills. And never ten degrees in a direction you want. Hotter in the summer. Colder in the winter. And smoggier than anything you'll find in the entire area. The sky was so hazy, I could barely see the hills I knew were just a few miles away.

I got out of my car, grabbed my crap, clicked my fob, and headed in. Sweat was already pouring down my back and it was a three-story walk-up. I guess the good news is that if anyone tried to attack me, they'd collapse from climbing all the stairs before they had a chance to kick down my door.

I put the key into the lock and had to shoulder the door open. The place smelled of fresh paint, which was good. One of Trovac's people had left the A/C on for me, but the heat was so intense, it was a lost cause. I used my boot to kick the door closed behind me. I nodded in appreciation at the two dead bolts, the slide lock, and the solid metal door. Wasn't sure if it was because the elf had made arrangements or if this apartment complex had already seen its share of crime and passion. I had a feeling it was more likely the latter.

The apartment had hardwood floors. Fucking hardwood floors. I know everyone and their mother is all into the hardwood floors, but when you're having to hide out from bad guys, the squeaky boards can be a life-and-death sort of thing. I mean, the bad guys will hear you coming unless a person can sprout wings like Graham. Speaking of which, I went and checked the windows. They had a simple lock at the top and I made a note to get security bars installed. I didn't need that bastard angel sneaking in like the tooth fairy to knock my teeth out in the middle of the night.

There was a small kitchen with a low breakfast bar. Does anyone ever use a breakfast bar for anything other than gathering junk mail? The kitchen was small, but I wasn't much of a cook, so that worked. At least it had a refrigerator, which is actually a luxury in Los Angeles. Most times you have to bring one yourself. I found a place of honor for Mom's Tupperware in the cabinet. She'd be happy to hear it was the first thing I did to make my home away from home feel like a home.

There was a small dining area with a card table and a chair. They were sort of situated under a brass chandelier that hadn't quite been centered correctly. I had to dodge one of the shiny arms as I walked past. The bathroom featured a white Formica countertop flecked with gold and low-flow faucets that spat out so little water, the lime-clogged streams almost evaporated in the heat before hitting my hands.

And the bedroom featured a low, twin-sized air mattress on the floor.

That was the entirety of my place.

I threw my plastic grocery bags down and was about to pull out all of the terrible outfits Trovac had picked out for me, but then figured rumpled-and-ready was far better camouflage than pressed-and-polished. Easy game.

I lay back on the air mattress with nothing to keep my brain busy but me and my thoughts. I wondered what Killian was up to. I wondered if Mom and Dad had told him what was going down. I wondered if Trovac let him know. My original plan was to put together some sort of crack team of specialists to get that queen of his out of her thrall, but thus far, the bad guys had me on the run and I wasn't able to do anything to address the issue.

I rolled over on my side. I wondered if Killian was thinking of me. If he had finished cleaning out M&K Tracking. If the office was now sitting empty and abandoned. What had happened to his basement apartment now that he was going to have to spend all his time in the elfin forest? Should I have gone and stayed with him?

I rolled onto my other side.

It was so strange I was thinking so much about him. It

was like, now that I had a moment of quiet, there was this sadness I didn't know was there, and now it was everywhere.

I rolled onto my back and stared at the ceiling.

If he was here, at least we could have hurled insults at each other or played a game of "What Stupid Thing Is About To Come Out Of Killian's Mouth" or something.

I put my arm over my eyes. This was stupid. I'd get up in the morning and go to work. Figure out what was going on so I could be free of Trovac. And then have time to think about Killian and the queen and what was ahead. This was just for now, until I could figure out a way for us out of this mess.

But my brain had other ideas. Round and round it spun about how much I had fucked up. I couldn't get my thoughts to calm down. I kept seeing the queen suspended in midair, her body feeding into the Dark Dimension portal. That moment of finding Killian in the prison completely wrecked. The slime that crawled up the Mother Tree. Trovac's black veins.

I rolled the whole six-inches off of the air mattress to the ground and started doing sit-ups. Then push-ups. Then stretching out. Then shadowboxing. I was trapped in this fucking hole with not even a television set to distract me. I couldn't go outside because I might be spotted. I needed something to eat, but hated everything I brought with me. I did a couple burpees and kept going until my muscles gave out.

I hopped into the shower, but by the time I got out, the sun was still up and I still had nothing to do.

This hiding out thing sucked. It sucked so bad. My brain was not a safe neighborhood to hang out in alone.

CHAPTER TEN

So, unless you're some bigwig, you don't actually get to park your car on the actual studio lot. You have to battle it out for garage parking with the third-class citizens of Los Angeles. And, let's be honest here, as a Production Assistant, I was technically a fourth or fifth class citizen. It was amazing the mayor allowed folks like me in the city limits without having to shake a cowbell and announce my arrival with a "P.A.! P.A.!" so that the moguls could scatter before inhaling the wafting scent of unwashed flannel, fast food, and stale cigarette smoke that usually accompanied my kind.

I walked towards the entrance. There was a terra-cotta wall around the entire movie lot. And if one wall wasn't enough, there was another wall in front of the wall made up by a tall, box hedge. A twenty-foot gate with a metal privacy screen flanked either side of the road, ready to be closed like some sort of medieval fortress if a horde of angry extras decided to storm the castle. And this was just one of the smaller lots that the studio owned.

I stepped forward to the security guard in his little white booth. He looked at my badge, checked my name on a list, rifled through my bag, and made me walk through a metal detector.

"First day here?" he asked with an overly welcome smile.

I tried to return his cheer. "Can hardly wait to get started!"

"Have a great day!" he said with a salute.

I stepped onto the lot and immediately recognized the area as a place I'd seen in dozens movies and TV shows. A golf cart with two rough looking guys drove past me. I found myself wishing I had a golf cart to drive around. Instead, I just trudged forward through the maze of buildings and tried to find the movie hanger where I was supposed to report for duty.

There were trailers all over the place filled with costumes and extras getting their duds for the day. There was a girl in tears who couldn't have been older than twenty-two, and a line of barely legal teenagers watching her cry with a combination of sympathy and fear.

"What do you mean I'm cut because I don't fit the costume?" she wept as she handed the outfit back. "I'm a size four!"

A large-breasted woman with curly, blonde hair and leathery skin croaked from inside the trailer, "Sorry. Maybe a little less time at Craft Services and you'll 'retain less water.' Lose twenty pounds, sweetie, and quit lying about your measurements."

"I'm a four!"

Seriously, she was a size four. I know because I could have fit four of her into one of my pant legs.

But the costume lady was having none of it and waved at the next person in line like she was some sort of anointed queen ushering through petitioners.

The extra girl turned and walked away. "How am I going to make rent..." she whispered under her breath, utterly devastated.

As much as it sucked, that wasn't the part that bugged

me. Listen, we all are hustling for rent. What creeped me out was that as she left, the costumer closed her watery eyes and smelled after the girl like she was inhaling the aroma of fresh baked bread. When she opened her eyes. there was this look of sated satisfaction on her face.

What sort of whackadoo person smells people's sadness? I mean, Los Angeles is filled with some kinky assed shit, but sniffing people's tears was a new one for me.

I kept going. It was hard to tell if this was the sadness eating stuff Trovac had been talking about or if I had just stumbled on some disturbing yet totally pedestrian fetish. It's hard to know with industry folks.

But I had my first day on the job to get to and getting fired at 8:00AM was not going to win me any favors. In fact, it was going to lose me a favor. I had a deadline and unfortunately, that was literal.

I turned the corner and there was Soundstage 13. How apropos. Actually, it was kind of weird that they had a Soundstage 13. These industry types tended to be super superstitious, and I had heard that 13 was usually banned from the backlot. And yet, here we were.

It looked like an airplane hanger. It was made out of white metal and the roof was curved. There were big sliding doors on the front for when they needed to bring in large set pieces. I heard they were called "elephant doors" because back in the golden days of moviemaking, they needed to be large enough to bring in an elephant. Because sometimes they would bring in an elephant. Or at least that was what some guy trying to get lucky at a bar one night told me. He could have been full of shit. He did not get lucky.

There was a regular looking side door, though, for us elephantless folk. It had a flashing red light above it. I was just about to open it when a hand reached out and grabbed mine.

"Don't go in!" hissed a hipster who looked barely old

enough to drive. His curly brown hair was tussled in that I-woke-up-this-way (…after an hour of adding product.) He had a flannel shirt he had tied around his waist to better show off his t-shirt, which was so tight it was practically painted onto his emaciated body. His jeans were so skinny, I don't know how he sat down without permanently reassigning himself to a higher section of the choir.

"I work here…" I explained, completely mystified.

He pointed up at the light and glared at me over his dark, horn-rimmed glasses. "They are taping. You go in there when that red light is flashing and your ass is grass."

I squinted at him. "Did you really just say 'ass is grass'?"

"I wanted to use a phrase someone of your generation would understand."

Out of deference to the effort my host had made to give me a low profile, I refrained from giving this ass a physical demonstration of what becoming grass was. Instead I gave him a sweet, sickly smile. "Of course. It's my first day. In fact, I've never even been a P.A. before."

"So who'd you sleep with to get this job?" he asked snidely.

I couldn't understand what this kid's issue was. "Excuse me?"

He looked me up and down and sighed. "Just wait until the light goes off."

"Who are you?"

"Chaz," he said, sucking off a long draw from the frozen smoothie he was carrying. "Also known as 'The Director'."

He pushed up his probably medically unnecessary thick-rimmed glasses with his middle finger and then walked away like he was all cool and shit, which was so completely cool with me, I can't even begin to describe how cool it was. What a jerk.

I folded my arms across my chest and stared at that

gawddamned flashing light, just daring it to go off.

So, here's the thing. I had heard that these backlots were actually filled with some of the nicest people you'll ever meet. Everyone is so flippin' happy to be working. Everyone is, at the very least, polite to one another because the jerk you blow off one day becomes the jerk you're blowing for a job the next.

So this guy, being as big an ass as he was, ESPECIALLY if he was the director, just struck me as weird. Between him and the costume lady, my "Something ain't right" meter was blinking off the scale.

The light finally stopped and I could hear the sound of a bell clanging from somewhere inside. I opened up the door only to find a room covered in gray sound blankets and ANOTHER big metal door. I opened that one and walked into the soundstage. I heard someone shout, "ROLLING" and the bell clanged again.

I told myself to tiptoe. The ceiling was a million miles above the ground and covered all in wood. The sets were not just nailed into the ground, they were suspended from the rafters, too, by long, aircraft cable. Painted on the perimeter of the floor was this big yellow line about four feet from the wall. It seemed like it made a clear path all the way to the far corner of the soundstage. I spotted what looked like the production office in the middle section and decided that was probably where I ought to be. I walked over, but slowed down as I passed by a bulletin board.

In addition to the call sheets and standard OSHA bullshit, there was a flier. At the very top was a header with a torch and the monogram "BLAA."

"BLAA..." I muttered under my breath. "Bringers of Light Association of America, huh?"

"That's a cut!" I heard someone shout in the far distance and the sound of the bell going off again. A black, bald-headed guy with a clipboard wandered out of his office. From the cut of his jib, he looked like someone who was used to hauling heavy things around. He wore jeans, thick boots, and a jacket. As a massive blast of industrial A/C kicked in, I understood why. He looked me up and down.

"Molly Mackie?" he said.

I shivered as I remembered that was my name now. "Present and accounted for."

"Follow me," he replied as he walked away, not really even pausing to see if I was following or not. "My name's Jeff. 1st AD." He handed me a call sheet without even pausing to see if he was holding it out in the general direction of my hands. I had to skip around to the side to grab it. He kept talking. "Memorize people's names and faces as quick as you can and you'll be in great shape."

I heard the sound of muffled crying coming from behind one of the set walls. "Is that person okay?" I asked.

He rolled his eyes. "Trudy Mellon."

"As in the fruit?" I asked.

"Sounds the same. As in the rich family that created some of America's finest universities, libraries, and institutions of learning." He held up his hand to stop me when I looked like I was about to be impressed. "She's not related. It's just a way to get called in by the casting directors who don't know any better." A loud wail interrupted him and he heaved another sigh. "Tough day shooting, but she'll be fine. If she was really upset she'd be crying in her trailer. Crying on-set means she's just looking for attention."

I couldn't believe he was so callous. "Are you sure? I can talk to her. I'm good at those sorts of things." I actually am not. At all. But figured there was no need to be a jerk about it.

He shrugged. "It's her morning routine."

"Morning routine?"

"Every day."

"Every day?! Doesn't that seem like maybe this is a

problem that should be addressed?"

"Listen, sweetie," said Jeff, lowering his clipboard. He waved in the direction of the set and explained it to me like I was a little kid finding out what hamburgers are made out of. "Directors set the tone for their set. This is a tough role that demands a lot of emotional realism. Chaz feels that keeping the actors emotionally raw gets a better performance. Don't worry about it. She's earning enough for the therapy." He put his arm around my shoulder. "You however, are not. So keep your head low."

Dare I say that it felt like this guy might actually be looking out for me?

"Thanks," I replied.

He tapped the top of my head with his clipboard. "If I can give you one piece of advice, you're everybody's friend and you never pick sides."

"I'm good at not picking sides," I replied.

"Then you're going to do just fine."

He walked me into the office and handed me a stack of paper. "These all need to go to payroll." He grabbed a paper map and circled where we were and where I needed to go. "Don't get lost," he said.

I took it and gave him a salute. "Aye, aye."

Unfortunately, even if you really seem to be getting along with your sergeant, sometimes a soldier needs to disobey a direct order.

CHAPTER ELEVEN

I saw the first monster as I was turning the corner to the commissary. There are many things you can say about the advances in modern plastic surgery, but no one is able to pull skin that tight. The poor woman's face was practically yanked behind her ears. I instinctively reached for my gun, and then reminded myself that I didn't get to carry around a gun anymore. Instead, I had a dumb wooden stake, on account of the metal detector, which was tucked into the top of my boot, which was about three-feet closer to the ground than I ever liked to have any particular weapon.

It gave me the heebie-jeebies to be so flipping defenseless. All I had was the spreadsheets Jeff gave me, and what was I going to do with those against some angry, charging beast? Death by a thousand paper cuts? It is really a slow way to go.

I turned my head to the side like I was fascinated by the papers in my hands... you know... in a manner that involved shielding my face. The last thing I needed was someone to alert the Other Side folks that the Mighty Maggie MacKay had been spotted on the studio lot in a cheap knockoff shirt that Goodwill would have rejected.

That's when I ran smack into Graham.

As the angel looked at me with his dead, brown eyes, the blood in my veins froze ice cold. My heart began pounding a million beats a minute and my throat went completely dry. All he had to do was grab me and I was toast. All he had to do was get me to cause a ruckus and I was toast. I had a favor I owed Trovac and a deadline looming. All Graham had to do was interrupt my ability to fulfill the favor and the magic of the fae people would put me away more permanently than he ever could.

"What the fuck are you doing here?" I asked at him, unable to keep myself from taking a step back in fear.

He gave me a smirk. God, I wanted to wipe it off his face with my knuckles. And he was still wearing his stupid leather trench coat. Who wears a leather trench coat in the middle of flipping August?

"Looked like you were lost, Maggie," he said. But then I noticed that he was sort of skootching away from me the same way I was skootching away from him.

I decided to play it tough. "You can't just come flying onto the lot, asshole," I said, waving my ID tag at his face. "They're really tight with security here."

He shrugged, throwing his words at me like we were ten-year-olds scrapping on a playground. "Yeah, I can."

So, technically, yes… he could. I had absolutely no idea how he had gotten this far in life without getting himself pulled from the tracker list what with all the rules he broke.

"Why are you here?" I asked his dumb face.

"I fucking work here," he said, pulling out an ID tag from his own shirt and waving it in my dumb face. "What's your problem?"

I licked my dry lips. "So, the Bringers of Light own this place, do they?" I asked.

His face paled. "What? There are Bringers of Light here?"

Something sooo didn't add up.

"That's who you work for, right?" I clarified for him, in case he had forgotten that whole open-up-a-portal-to-the-Dark-Dimension-in-the-name-of-the-Bringers-of-Light incident we were both witness to, like, just a couple days ago.

"No!" he said, like I had aligned him with the spawn of Satan. Which really wasn't that far of a stretch for this asshole. "I just work here!"

"Wait, but… you broke out of jail…"

"You're right. I broke out of jail. So that I wouldn't ever have to go BACK to that jail. I WORK here now," he said, like I was the biggest idiot.

"You're not here to haul me in?"

"NO! Fuck no, Maggie." He looked at me. "Are you here to haul ME in?"

I stared him right back unblinking. "Nooo…"

We stood there staring at each other a little longer, both still completely flabbergasted.

"Sooo… we literally just ran into each other?" I clarified.

"I needed to get out of the Other Side and this is where my contact planted me."

"No chance your contact was elfin?" I said, ready to kick some ass MacKay style if Trovac was playing both sides.

"Um… the elves are not exactly my friends right now."

"Right. On account of you putting their leader in thrall."

"I was struggling to make ends meet. But I'm trying to set it right, okay?"

"You have got to be kidding me," I replied, barely able to contain my eye roll. "After a whole, what, three days you've reformed and are now flying the straight and narrow?"

"No. I'm not," he answered. He looked at me like I was the stupidest idiot ever. "But those Light Bringers left me in the jail to rot, which was something they weren't supposed to do. And let me tell you, you don't double-cross this double-crosser or you'll find yourself crossed out."

"Wow, Graham," I replied. "Are you a poet?"

"Shut up, Maggie. I'm just trying to figure out how to go back home, because right now I'm pretty sure the Shadow Elves are going to assassinate me whenever I go to the grocery store. But then I find myself running into you and now it looks like I'm gonna have to put up with your ass fucking things up."

"You're going to be the one fucking things up," I shot back at him.

We stood there for another moment glaring at each other. He was the first one to blink.

"What if this was divine intervention?" he posed, like it was some sort of legitimate theory I should spend more than half-a-second considering.

"There is no god on your side."

"No, listen, Maggie. We could fucking help each other and shit."

"Watch your mouth, angel," I said, walking away. "You sure do cuss a lot."

He fell in step beside me. "What? You a goodie-two-shoes all the sudden?"

I stuck my nose in the air. "I'm not the one who needs to uphold the reputation of being one of the gods' chosen ones."

"You should reconsider that," he said, adjusting his package.

"You're so gross."

"I'm just saying, did you ever wonder why everyone is always coming after you, Maggie?" He dropped it like it was some great big tasty morsel and I should start begging for him to tell me more.

"Because I'm the best World Walker folks can hire since my dad retired?"

"You ain't that good," he said, giving me the side-eye.

"I seem to have no trouble keeping up with you."

"Last I checked, I'm not the one who needed to bust himself out of jail."

"Listen, how is a guy supposed to fight the chick who's the talk of all the ancient vampire texts?"

This time I looked at him like he was the idiot. "What?!"

"Oh, didn't that dumb priest of yours or that taekwondo reject drop that info dump on you yet?"

"First off, Xiaoming is Chinese, not Korean. Second off, no," I replied, crossing my arms and challenging him to go on. "I'm afraid that they left that little part out."

He shrugged and started to act like now HE was going to walk away. "You should ask them about it sometime."

Here's the thing. These angels? They've got the "armor of God" protecting their heart and their gonads. But their wing joints? It's kind of like an Achilles' heel. A feathery Achilles heel. I reached out and punched him right between the shoulder blades.

"FUCK! OW!" he cried, clutching at his back.

I grabbed his wing under his overcoat where I knew it would be and felt the bone bending in my two hands. "You're going to tell me what, exactly, you know or I am going to snap your wing like a wishbone."

"Gawddammnit, Maggie…"

"Watch your mouth."

"This fucking hurts. Let go of me and I'll tell you everything I know."

I just bent the wing more.

"FINE! Fine. There's a text that says you're going to destroy the vampires. That's all I know."

I let him go and dusted off my hands. "That's all you had to say. Why do you have to go making things difficult?"

"I like being manhandled by you," he lied, glaring at me and rubbing his wing ruefully.

"So why would the Bringers of Light be after me if I'm

the one person who could bring down the vampires?"

"First, because you were also the only one alive rumored to be strong enough to heal up the rift they were making. But now because things got fucked up and you know who was behind it, you and the vampires are on the same side. You are an enemy of each other's enemy, and do you know what that makes you?"

I didn't want to say it. But I did. "Frienemies?"

"Bingo. You and the vampires, teamed up to take down the Bringers of Light. They might be able to fight one of you, but both of you? They fucked up taking you down and now they gotta fight you both. So, you know what that means, Maggie?"

"No."

"Everybody wants you dead."

CHAPTER TWELVE

I swore under my breath that as soon as I delivered the paperwork to HR, I was going to give Father Killarney a little call and discuss some of the fine print of recent goings-on that he may have left out of his beer-swilling sermons.

Was that why everyone was really so hell-bent on killing me? You'd think they'd have figured out from pretty much every single fucking movie ever made that the surest way to make sure a prophecy happened is to try to prevent it. Shit. Even I knew that and I didn't even have a college degree.

I found the HR department. It was a white, two story building with white, paned glass. There were some big flowering bushes in the front my mom probably could have identified. Inside, there was some gray, industrial carpet and gray, industrial office furniture. There was also a row of chairs and six people fighting back tears.

I walked up to the receptionist who stared at me with dull eyes. "Yes?"

"I'm supposed to drop these off..." I replied, glancing over my shoulder.

"You're new here, aren't you?" she yawned.

"Yeah."

She pointed to a big box filled with paperwork. "Leave it there. I'll handle it."

From the size of the stack already there, I wasn't so sure. And it was confirmed by one of the gals sitting in a chair.

"You said you would handle time sheets last week!" she exclaimed. "I'm getting evicted because you haven't sent my check!"

"It was merely a clerical error," droned the secretary.

"You're the clerk!" the woman replied.

"Payroll must have sent your check to the wrong address. Please wait patiently and someone will be with you shortly."

I walked out of the office and back onto the wide street of the studio lot and wondered what the hell was going on. It was like everywhere I turned, everyone was having a lousy day. I mean, sure, the studios has issues and politics like any normal workplace, but this was a dream factory for all the people employed. Rule #1 in Hollywood is that you never let people see how you really feel, especially at work. But everyone here was Crabby McCrabberpants.

I got back to the soundstage and Jeff was standing next to a table, filling out more paperwork. He had a walkie-talkie strapped to his belt and an earpiece in one ear. He finished saying something into the mic, which was found on the wire running from his ear down to the walkie-talkie, and then released the "Listen to me! I'm talking!" button and shook his head.

"Man, people are in a bad mood around here..." I remarked.

"Everybody wants something," he replied, without even looking up. "And sometimes you can't always get what you want." He finished filling out the numbers with a flourish and then stood up, cracking his broad back. "Ready for your next task?"

"Am I ever!" I exclaimed with mock excitement. I even threw in a happy little air punch to accentuate how much I meant it.

Jeff motioned for me to follow him and I fell in step. "This is going to be your most important task of the day. It is absolutely imperative that you listen carefully and take notes. If this is not done right, it is not only your ass on the line and my ass on the line, but the entire production will be placed at risk. Do you have a phone?"

I pulled out the one Trovac gave me. Figured this sounded like as big of an "emergency usage only" as a person could get.

Jeff took it out of my hands, typed in his number, texted himself, and handed it back to me. "You never turn your phone off. If you see me calling, you drop everything and answer it. Got it?" I nodded, completely freaked out by his urgency. He handed me a clipboard and a stack of papers. "Now write this down," he replied and then explained. "You keep the battery on your phone for when I need to get a hold of you. No playing games or scrolling through Facebook. If the battery dies, you die. Write everything I'm about to say on paper. Better yet, tattoo it on your arm."

This was serious. From the look in his eye, I was getting the gravity of the situation. I nodded in acknowledgment. I was going to be his Girl Friday on this. We walked out of the soundstage and up the rickety aluminum steps to a large trailer fitted with brown faux-wood paneling and bench seats.

Whoever hung out here was a big deal. There was a bed on one end and a bathroom and a fully equipped kitchen on the other and he had the entire place to himself.

Jeff pointed at the counter at a tall, industrial blender. "The director needs his juice."

CHAPTER THIRTEEN

I stood there, shoving another carrot into the feeder-tube, and pressed the button. I was a gawddamned juicer. I. Maggie MacKay. The Best World Walker this side of the Other Side was stuck blending fruit smoothies for some twenty-eight year old asshole who barely graduated from USC.

The good news is that making juice gave me lots of time to think and mull things over and figure out next steps.

Jeff came back with the glass I had just poured, almost untouched. I could see the look on his face.

"What?" I asked.

"Chaz said there was too much pulp."

I looked down at the glass, the green gloop inside sticking to the sides. "Are you fucking kidding me?" I said. "I made it exactly as the recipe stated."

"You're going to need to blend it longer," said Jeff, wiping away the sweat from his smooth scalp nervously. "He has an irritable bowel and this will give him gas."

I thought of how I'd be happy to rip him a few new exhaust ports and sighed. I picked up the glass and moved to pour it back into the blender. Jeff grabbed my hand.

"What are you doing?" he asked, horrified.

"I'm blending his smoothie," I replied with absolutely no idea why the man was freaking out so much.

"You can't just re-blend the smoothie," he said. "You need to make it fresh. From scratch. Again."

"He won't know the difference."

"Listen, Maggie," he said, his voice low. "I'm protecting your ass here. I owe that fat elf a favor, and the favor he called in was that I get you this gig and I don't let you get fired."

My mouth went dry. Rule #1 of The Other Side is that there is no Other Side. You don't just go talking to people about what you are and what you do unless you are absolutely, positively sure that you are among friends. And here Jeff was blowing his cover? AND he knew my interdimensional immigration sponsor? "First off, my name is Molly and second off, you know Trovac?"

"How the hell do you think a lowlife reject like yourself got this job, MAGGIE?"

I bit back several words I wanted to say about how I got this job, including saving the universe from implosion, giving up my entire life to make sure at least one World Walker skipped out on getting turned into a concrete statue, and being solely responsible for making sure that Jeff slept safely at night as opposed to finding monsters in his closet, but instead just smiled. "So, what you're saying is that if I get fired, you die?"

He pointed his finger at me. "Don't even play."

"So, what you're saying is that you have a vested interest in me doing really well at this job?" I pressed the button on the blender with delight.

"Maggie," he warned taking my hand off the machine. "Things are not right here. Things, in fact, are completely fucked. I have worked really, really hard to get where I am. I'm going to need you to rein it in so that neither of us ends up dead."

I sighed. The guy was doing me a solid. I banged the blender's contents into the trashcan and shoved a banana into the empty container. "I may have noticed that things here are a little FUBAR. And that's actually why I've been sent." Figured I didn't need to let him in on the little fact I had not been "sent", I had been "placed", and there was a favor hanging over my head, too.

"Maggie, Other Siders are dying here. As in, they are dying right and left. We could film a whole zombie apocalypse flick and not have to rent out a single mannequin with all the spare bodies I've been finding around this place. And that's just folks I'VE found. Who knows how many more there are."

"What?" I said. I mean, I don't read the newspaper often, but the press would have a field day with these sorts of shenanigans. "No, that's not possible. We would have heard about it."

"You think I'm making this up?" His eyebrows shot up so high, his whole bald scalp became his forehead. "Why would I make something like this up?"

I pressed the blender button. "There are rules about these sorts of things. Other Siders can't just go around killing people."

"Listen, maybe for folks in the union. But nonunion? Shoot, they are fair game and Firebrand Studios has declared it open season."

"Surely someone—"

"Maggie, you don't get it, do you? The Other Siders here? They're on the run. They're looking for a jobs and keeping their heads low. They're not going to make a bunch of noise. It would alert the authorities to the fact that certain members of the staff don't seem to have any record of graduations, vaccinations, marriages, birth certificates, you name it, prior to just a few weeks before they began working here. You think anyone wants that sort of attention?"

"But if they don't renew their work permit," I pointed

out, "someone like me is going to come looking for them and find out that they're dead."

"Maggie, the only people who care about that are the World Walkers. And it seems like the World Walkers lose people all the time."

Stan, I thought. Fucking Stan, the president of the guild. Of COURSE these people were being lost. He was making sure to lose them. AND he was turning all the World Walkers into marble statues so that there wouldn't even be anyone around to help even if someone DID happen to notice.

Jeff was still talking. "They leave set and things just happen. And everyone at their funeral talks about how nice it was that they realized a dream before they ended up dead. Or they develop an allergy to the sun. Or the people leave one day and they show up the next and just aren't quite the same. Their eyes have a golden glint to them when you look at them out of the corner of your eye and I find a corpse which is the dead ringer for someone I just talked to five minutes earlier."

"Golden glint? Allergy to the sun?" I repeated, just to make sure I had followed everything he had said correctly. "You're saying that this studio is run by monsters?"

"Yeah, " said Jeff, tasting the smoothie I finished and pouring it in the trash. "That's exactly what I'm saying. More turmeric, less pulp."

CHAPTER FOURTEEN

Jeff switched off his walkie-talkie and pulled the earpiece out of his ear. He walked over to the door, shut it, and then sat down on the couch. He wiped his face with both hands. "Listen, when I got here, this was the best job I ever had. I had just emigrated from the Other Side—"

"What are you?" I asked.

"Fawn," he replied.

"What?"

"Prosthetic boots take care of the hoof issue and I've got one hell of a waxer in Korea Town."

"Can I get her name?"

"Let her know I sent you and she'll give me $50 off my next session."

"Done."

"So," he continued, "I started working here and it was great. You know this studio!" He held up both his hands as if in worship of all the awesomeness. "They are the keepers of all the great films in history. All the movies I grew up loving as a kid! This is THE studio everyone wants to work for. And then things began to happen..."

"What things?"

"We got that new group of shareholders. Seemed like it was going to be a perfect fit at the time, but..." he ran his hand over his dark, bald head. "They're doing all these reboots. They started taking the films I loved and folks I knew loved and then redoing them. The first one hits in just a couple weeks and it is terrible. Let me tell you, I've been working on the sets. I've been sitting in the editing rooms. It's like... Okay, it's like this. They're creating these auto-tuned pop stars and then plugging them into the starring roles in these reboots and then having them sing and dance... You know that movie The Hitman?" he asked.

"It's a classic," I replied. It was a tragic boxing movie about this Latino guy forced to fight in fixed games. Came out in the 1970s and won a bunch of Oscars. The stunts were incredible at the time. It was dark and gritty and artistic. "What about it?"

"They turned it into a musical."

"What?"

"Hand to the gods, a musical. And not like a Les Mis musical. Like an aimed-at-13-year-old-girls on network television musical. With a happy ending that involves fireworks and jazz hands."

"Now, there's a place for happy endings and jazz hands..." I said, trying to play devil's advocate.

"They didn't bother filming below the waist because they are going to CGI all the dance moves."

"CGI tap dancing?"

"CGI tap dancing."

"So you're saying they're TRYING to make every film student in the nation want to burn Firebrand Studios down?"

"I think that's what they want."

I really didn't know how much he knew vs. how much I knew, so I decided to play dumb and see which dots he could connect for me. "What do you mean?"

"I think this studio feeds on unhappiness, Maggie."

"What?"

"It seems like if they can take something that people know and love and destroy it, it makes them stronger. It feeds them."

I'm sure my eyes looked as huge as the two oranges I was peeling to put in the blender. "They feed on unhappiness?"

"It's like... it's like they are vampires of EMOTION."

"This is not good."

"Creatures evolve, Maggie. I got this theory. I think sucking blood is completely 1800s. I'm thinking the new craze is sucking unhappiness. THAT's what these shareholders are all about."

"You're saying that there is a newly developed species of vampire and every time someone gets cranky, they get food?"

"That's exactly what I'm saying. And I'm saying they are in charge of this studio."

I whirred the blender for a moment while I thought. I absentmindedly stroked my hand against the scars on my neck and missed my neckguard all over again. "But is that such a bad thing?" I asked. "I mean, they're not killing people for food. They're just sucking off the bad feelings."

"Have you found yourself walking around recently and thinking about things that make you sad? Thinking about people you miss? Thinking about the way things should have been?"

I thought back to last night where I couldn't get my brain to stop spinning about Killian and the queen and how I had ruined everything. "Yeah."

"That's THEM. I'm sure of it! And they are growing. And I'm thinking this studio may have found a way to broadcast this control. Imagine if vampires were able to suck your blood every time you picked up a magazine on a newsstand."

"That wouldn't be good."

"Well, it's like that except with your feelings. These

emotion vampires go spewing hate on the news and they fill magazines and advertisements with stuff that makes people feel lousy. And they just keep hammering it home and hammering it home how awful everything is. I'm convinced they're creating depression in people. Clinical, psychological, physiological depression. All these people dying here? Coroner always says it is suicide brought about by depression, but they're not depressed, Maggie. They're under attack. They're nothing but feed bags for these monsters. And you know what happens when an Other Sider offs themselves here, while under attack?"

"What?"

"They got just enough magic in their souls that remembers where they came from, and the magic wants to get back to the Other Side. It creates a hole in the boundary. Just a little hole. But a hole for the Other Side to come bleeding through. All these little pinpricks, it's just a matter of time before everything comes crashing down."

"But they..." I stopped myself and then realized I needed to let Jeff in on the stuff I knew. "There's this group. I know they are here. They're called the Bringers of Light. I saw their logo on some letterhead hanging on your OSHA board."

Jeff furrowed his brow and crossed his arms as he took what I was saying in. "BLAA? I thought they were just third-party vendors the studio hired for HR and payroll and stuff."

"They are turning World Walkers into marble statues and they are trying to destroy the elves."

His eyes got wide. "That ain't good."

"No," I replied. "'That ain't good.' So how do you think they fit in with these emotional suckers that are these new shareholders or came with these new shareholders or whatever?"

He paused for a little while to noodle it through and then seemed to have an idea. "World Walkers could seal up the holes," he guessed. "As for the elves..." Jeff stopped for a second just to double-check his walkie-talkie. "Elves have glamour."

"I feel like Hollywood is glamorous enough on its own."

"No, listen, if these emotional vampires need people to stay fixated on what they are getting ready to unleash with this wave of reboots, they need something that will cause people to stay entranced with the bullshit they're spewing. Because, listen, folks are getting wise. They're turning off the news. They're putting down the magazines. They're disconnecting from the Internet and not sharing the downer posts online. These new vampires need something to get people to pay attention. And that's what the elves can do with their glamour that no other creature can do. And if they can bleed off the elves' power, that energy has to go somewhere."

"Huh?"

"Einstein's whole thing that energy cannot be created or destroyed. It can only change forms. What if these Bringers of Light have made some sort of an agreement to bring that energy here or something? Maybe there's like... through a vortex or something. If they can destroy the elves, the boundaries between The Dark Dimension, The Other Side, and Earth merge into one. And the Dark Dimension is not exactly the cheeriest place in three dimensions. These new vampires will have all the food they can shove into their gobs."

I stopped him right there. "But why would they be at war with the regular vampires?"

"I dunno, Maggie. Maybe competition for food sources? Team Kill by Draining Their Blood vs. Team Kill by Draining Their Souls? There are only so many people and there are more and more vampires coming every day."

"So... we just need to kill the vampires," I said, pouring the finished glop of green smoothie into the sippy cup for the director. "I'm good with killing vampires."

Jeff began to laugh. "Maggie, if you can figure out who they are and can do it without drawing attention to who we are and what we are doing here, have at it. But what do you think I've been doing?"

"You've been fighting this fight?" I asked. "A faun?" Fauns are lovers rather than fighters. They prefer to frolic through the fields with big-breasted women and well-hung men. It takes a lot to get a faun to fight.

"They came after my husband," Jeff said. His jaw twitched. "His was the first body I found. He was never depressed or suicidal. Someone made him do it. And I was willing to sell my soul to an elf to avenge him."

CHAPTER FIFTEEN

Jeff flicked on his walkie-talkie and put in his earpiece. "Sorry for being off-line!" he said. "What was that?" I heard a voice come across the line and Jeff pulled away. I could hear the shouting from across the room. He sighed and then replied, "Roger that. On my way with the smoothie."

He held up the cup in a toast. "To not getting fired today, Maggie."

I held up a banana, suddenly realizing just how important it was that I not screw this up. "To not getting fired."

The door closed behind him and I finished whirring the fruit and putting it into little sealed to-go sippy cups in the refrigerator. Jeff had stuck his head out for me and that meant something. It felt like no one had really done that on a regular basis, except Killian.

I was washed in a wave of sadness, but this time I understood what was going on. And somehow, just knowing I was being manipulated cut off the feelings like a door in a water chute. I mean, sure, there was still a little dripping around the edges, but it wasn't the torrent.

I walked over to the door, flung it open, and poked my head out to see who had been trying to open up one of my psychic veins.

I saw a familiar mop of blonde curls sashaying down the street, cigarette clutched between her sausage fingers and cankles jammed into an uncomfortable looking pair of mules.

Anyone who's ever worked on a set will tell you the costume and makeup people are the only ones you can trust. Everyone else will be looking out for themselves, but Wardrobe and Makeup are always on your side.

"Double-whammy, huh?" I muttered at her. Let the talent think they have a trusted friend to confide in and then knock 'em from behind.

I realized my hand was still running along the scars on my neck. At least with a vampire, you could see it coming, you could defend yourself. How the hell does a person defend themselves against a psychic attack?

I walked back into the soundstage, but didn't even have a chance to think because I walked straight into a heated conversation.

Chaz was standing there glaring at Jeff, who was looking back at him with apologetic eyes. The director sucked his green smoothie through his straw in disappointment.

"I didn't know I should pack up before the shoot!" whined some model-thin, nineteen-year-old chick. Her scrawny frame on her four-inch high heels teetered in the wind. For the record, there was no wind. Her eyes were vacant and glassy. She twirled her perfectly straightened, ombre-dyed hair. "I just had a lot to do this morning." Her bottom lip stuck out in a pout.

"Fix this," said Chaz, turning on his heel. "I've got a movie to shoot." And then he walked away.

Jeff waved me over as he smiled indulgently at the starlet. "It's no problem, Ms. D'rela. You just focus on your big scene today. We'll take care of everything." He turned to me, the fake smile glued across his face. "Maggie, would you mind going over to Ms. D'rela's hotel and getting her things together for her so she can catch her 4PM flight?"

I gritted my teeth and smiled back. "I'd be delighted."

Jeff handed me the key to her hotel room and steered her back towards set.

"Is she throwing me attitude?" I heard Ms. D'rela accuse as I walked away.

"No, no," excused Jeff. "She's just like that. Resting bitch face. You, fortunately, don't have that problem."

They were both lucky I didn't have time to show them the rest of my bitch face. I stalked off towards my car and heard my phone buzz in my pocket. I pulled it out and read the screen: "Pick up coffee." It was then filled with a list of six different variations of coffee infused drinks in various sizes. As I read, another text came in with three more. How the hell was one person supposed to carry someone's luggage plus nine cups of coffee in a shitty car? My phone buzzed and there was another text with four more orders. And then the note: "Front the money. We'll reimburse you. Make sure they all stay hot."

I considered just allowing myself to be hit by a bus while I crossed the street.

Pushing that to-do item to the bottom of the to-do list, I drove over to Ms. D'rela's schwanky hotel and pulled out in front. Seriously, I think the cost of one week here could've built me an entire house.

Carefully manicured palms flanked the doors in handcrafted terra-cotta pots. There was tile instead of concrete in the drive and a Spanish fountain tinkled near the entrance, despite the fact we were in the middle of a flippin' drought. Every time the door opened, a waft of welcome A/C flowed out of the lobby. The entire place smelled of industrial-strength, artesian cleaners.

The valet took one look at my beat-up beater of a beaten-down wreck and said, "You can't park here."

"I'm picking stuff up for Ms. D'rela," I replied.

He gave a sniff. "You'll need to pull around. To the back. To one of the farthest parking spaces."

I jammed my car into gear and lurched forward. How many times had I risked my life and limb for humanity's existence? How many times? And THIS was my thanks? I was considered so low on the scale, a valet literally turned down a payday when faced with handling my car. I considered just letting the Earth burn. But then I thought of Mindy and Austin and their baby and figured maaaaybe I should see things through for their sake.

I turned the corner and saw the rear entrance. There was a parking space the size of a postage stamp about three rows away. I backed in, threw my car into park, and carefully edged my way out, trying hard not to ding the car next to me with my door. I clicked the locks, but frankly, the worst thing that would have happened if someone stole my crap-mobile was that I would have to handwrite them a thank you note.

I strode into the hotel and pressed the elevator going up. It dumped me off on the fifth floor and I opened the door to Ms. D'rela's room. I walked in and once again considered my career path.

Her room was trashed. One night in the place and she had torn it apart. Her clothes were everywhere. Free samples of toiletries were everywhere. The mini-bar was emptied. Bottles of wine were scattered across the floor.

How the hell did one person destroy a place so utterly and completely in twenty-four hours? I mean, I'd get it if she had been battling out with some force of evil, but from the looks of things, her biggest battle was the lack of a hotel corkscrew.

I started scooping up her clothes, folding them, but making sure that they got a little wrinkle or two in the process, because if she wanted them to come out fresh as a daisy, she should have packed herself. Besides, she'd probably just have her maid dump everything off at the dry cleaner and it wouldn't even matter.

As I was rolling everything up in a generally packed manner, I reached down and felt a zing.

"GAWDDAMMNIT!" I said, yanking my hand back and sticking my finger in my mouth. It felt like a mousetrap had closed on it. Did this crazy bitch go around setting mousetraps around her room to keep the maids from trying on her stuff?

I knelt down and lifted the bed skirt. There was a single, dangly pair of earrings lying tangled in a used pair of underwear.

"Oh… you are not making me do this…" I groaned. "I am not getting paid enough for this…"

I went to the bathroom and grabbed the one clean washcloth she hadn't wadded up and left on the counter. I went back to the bed, trying to remind myself that Mindy was going to be having that baby soon and I was going to have to get used to dealing with unclean undergarments. Somehow, a loaded diaper paled in comparison to this bitch's unmentionables. But that zing I felt meant there was magic in Ms. D'rela's family jewels.

I picked up the underwear and shook the earrings out of it. Kind of a brilliant security system, if you asked me. Who would have ever looked for valuables in the dirty laundry? I certainly would not have if the fate of the world hadn't been at risk.

I tossed the underwear into the bag and picked up the jewelry, walking it over to the bathroom. I turned on the water in the sink and doused the earrings in cheap hotel shampoo, letting the water run until scalding.

After what seemed like the necessary amount of sterilization, I turned off the water and pulled the earrings out. The water had dissipated the magic just enough. It was building back up, but there was a slight check in the flow.

"Hello, beauties," I said, staring at their sparkling depths. "So, what do you do?"

CHAPTER SIXTEEN

I sat across from Xiaoming as he plopped down at the chrome Formica table. His blue terrycloth robe fell open to show a set of striped boxers and a stained wife-beater. Judging from what I could see, it looked like maybe he had put on some new socks beneath his open-toed slippers. But nothing else had changed. He had suffered a werewolf attack several months ago, and for whatever reason, decided to use that opportunity to return everything to exactly as it had been before.

It seemed kind of dumb to me at the time, but now? Now, I kind of got it. When it came time to hire my own real estate witch, I wondered if I'd do the same thing.

That said, my place was in slightly "more worthy to be restored" shape that this guy's. Every surface was covered in a dingy film of yellow tobacco smoke. The kitchen smelled of burned fish sauce from yesterday's dinner, old ginger, and tobacco smoke. Lit incense swirled around his little altar to the gods, the oranges and electric candles lost in the haze of his tobacco smoke. I guess there was more than one way to protect your home from intruders. Namely, asphyxiation.

I was bone tired. Between packing up the rest of the hotel, doing the coffee run, dropping Ms. D'rela off at the airport and hauling her bags around because her scrawny little bird arms couldn't lift her overnight bag, I was ready to just fall over and die. But, the thing was, if I didn't figure out what was going on, I might find myself in an involuntary position of falling over and dying. Although, every minute that passed in Xiaoming company made it a more and more welcome option.

I pulled the earrings out of my jacket pocket and unwrapped them from the napkin I stole from the lobby bar.

"Where you find this?" he glared at me as he sucked on his cigarette.

I waved away the smoke. "Xiaoming, don't you think you could give it a rest for like... the whole five minutes I'm here... I gotta wash my clothes every time I step through your door."

He responded by blowing his cloud in my direction. "The quicker you get this over, the quicker you get out."

"Right," I sighed, realizing that I was probably the reason why he went to such extraordinary efforts to make things so unpleasant every time I visited. "So, there was this model. She had me pack up her stuff and her earrings bit me when I tried to pick them up."

"They are magic," he replied with finality. "You go now."

"I know that," I said with a sigh, urging him to delve a little deeper into the encyclopedia of his mind. "I just need to know what kind of magic."

He ashed onto the carpet. "What do you think I am, Maggie? Some Google? Some library? How should I know?"

Sometimes even a Southern California girl like me knows when to turn on the Southern charm. What can I say? Sucking up on set was providing me with some real world tools for manipulating situations sans fists.

94

I shrugged with wide-eyed amazement that he was coming up empty. "It just seems like you know everything, Xiaoming. I just couldn't even imagine that you wouldn't know what these were. Nothing? You have no idea where I could get more information? I mean, there's no one who knows more about magic than you."

I almost batted my eyes, but decided that might be laying it on a little thick. Someone hand me a gawddamned Oscar already.

He grunted, catching my sideways compliment grudgingly. "Maybe I know place to look for information."

"That's all I'm asking," I replied with the gritted smile Jeff had taught me so well today. "I just want to know what they are."

He squinted his eyes at me sharply. "You think she will miss them if they are gone? These not prom jewelry from Fashion District."

I got up. "She had so much crap with her, I bet she didn't even know she packed them."

He nodded. "Leave them here. I find out for you."

I crossed over to the door. "Thanks, Xiaoming. Hey! Now that I'm a permanent resident of Los Angeles, we should do lunch."

"No."

"My people can call your people!" I said over my shoulder as I turned the handle.

"I do not want to hear from 'your people'."

"You'll never work in this town with that sort of attitude."

"That is my hope!" he shouted at me as I walked out.

I smiled. He was definitely my people.

The sun was long since gone as I walked over to my car and hopped onto the freeway back towards the Valley. Traffic wasn't great, but it wasn't awful, either.

I had survived my first big day on the job and no one got staked. It was a flipping miracle. I groaned as I

95

thought what waited for me back in my new apartment, though. Nothing but an air mattress and a couple bags of Doritos. I was tempted to pull my car through a drive-thru, but then thinking about my weekly allowance and how much I was getting paid at my job, I realized that wasn't in the cards this week. I'd just need to remember to steal some food from set tomorrow.

When I opened the door to my apartment, the lights were blazing and the smell of garlic and butter hit my nose. My mouth went from zero to drooling-on-the-carpet in three seconds flat.

"THE MIGHTY MAGGIE MACKAY HAS RETURNED!"

Pipistrelle jumped out of the kitchen with a paper towel wrapped around his waist. I shut the door behind me as quickly as possible, hoping no one out in the courtyard had been listening too hard.

"Pipistrelle?! What are you doing here?" I asked, completely dumbfounded to find my sister's brownie in my crappy apartment cooking me dinner.

"Trovac sent me! Said that the Mighty Tracker Maggie was in need!"

I did not even want to think about what my heavily pregnant sister was thinking about me poaching Pipistrelle at this stage in the game.

"Are you sure that's such a good idea...?" I asked, looking around nervously.

"You need me to save the world!" he said with a grin that went from ear-to-ear. "And so I shall! We shall save the world before you get yourself fired for not knowing—" He seemed to be trying very hard to remember the exact phrase. "'How to do a simple task without screwing it up and killing Jeff with your incompetence.' That is why I am here!"

As much of an asshole as Trovac was, man, I was happy to have Pipistrelle at my side. Just let one of those emotion vampires try to suck my soul tonight. Nothing could get me down. And from the garlic wafting through the place, the regular old vampires would get a run for their money, too.

"I accept your help and gratefully," I replied. I hung my jacket on the door handle of the coat closet. "Very, very gratefully. Because I'm pretty sure that Trovac is right. I'm going to screw this up."

CHAPTER SEVENTEEN

"Gawddamnit, Maggie," said Jeff. "What the hell did you do?"

I started backing away from the door. "Nothing…?"

He pointed at the phone. "I've got Ms. D'rela's agent on the phone yelling my ear off that either you are grossly incompetent and incapable of doing a simple task -OR- you stole stuff from her client's hotel room when you packed yesterday."

"I didn't!" I replied, thinking of the earrings I left with Xiaoming and knowing full well that I did.

"Well, did you happen to see a pair of earrings lying around and did you happen to pack them?"

"No…?" I lied.

Jeff wiped his face. "This is the last thing I need."

"Listen, Jeff," I explained. "Her room was trashed. Completely trashed. Maybe mention it to her agent that when I went in there, the place was a mess. I assumed she was just messy, but maybe someone tossed her room…?" I tried to put on my biggest, innocent doe eyes.

"Really?" he asked, his own face worried.

"Yeah," I replied. "Maybe it's something to bring up

with the hotel staff. I mean, I couldn't imagine her being that messy, but you never know with people, do you…"

He rubbed his sockets with his fists. "Hell…"

"Only if you have to deal with her."

That got just the slightest hint of a chuckle from him. Resigned, he pulled out some paper from his drawer. "Our insurance company is not going to be happy about this…"

"You mean 'her insurance company' isn't? The hotel has a policy," I reminded him. "If there was anything of value, it should have been put into the safe."

He pointed his finger at me, the lightbulb going off. "You're right."

"I am right."

"She won't care that you're right."

"Let them hash that out. It ain't our problem."

He leaned against his desk. "You better be telling me the truth about those earrings."

"Would I lie to you?" I asked.

He shook his head. "I'm pretty sure you would."

Smart guy. "So what adventures do we have on the docket for today?" I said, clasping my hands in front of me like an excited kindergarten teacher about to look at her students' art and crafts project. Because, seriously, with the quality of crap I saw pooped out yesterday on set? I was starting to think the kindergarten kids had a corner on talent.

He looked down at his clipboard, walked over to his filing cabinet, and pulled out a stack of papers.

"Have you ever heard of this thing called digital technology?" I remarked. "It saves trees."

"I'm not an elf," he replied. "Fuck the trees. We've got a movie to make."

Hollywood in a nutshell… And he was most certainly not an elf. Just as he was about to hand me a stack of green and blue carbon papers, he asked, "Did you make the director his juice?"

"I made the director his juice."

He seemed grateful I had managed to get one thing right on his list of things to take care of today. He passed over the stack. "I need you to run over to the prop warehouse and find out when they're finally going to get around to delivering these items." Someone squeaked something into his walkie-talkie and he pressed the button. "Roger that." He shook his head. "Duty calls."

"…how exactly do I do this?" I asked as I looked through the list.

"Figure it out!" he shouted over his shoulder as he walked away and started up a conversation with one of the gaffers.

"Great," I sighed.

My phone buzzed. I was beginning to learn that every time my phone buzzed it meant someone needed a new cup of coffee from some random artisan coffee shop a two-hour drive from the lot. But this time, it was a text message from Xiaoming. It read: Emergency. You call now.

I didn't even know the guy owned a phone much less how he managed to get my unlisted number on a pay-as-you-go plan. I was going to need to have a little chat with Trovac as soon as I got through with this conversation. I scrambled out of the soundstage and found myself a quiet corner by a potted plant.

"Hello?" I hissed into the receiver as soon as Xiaoming picked up.

"This Molly Mackie?"

It took a second to remember my pseudonym. "Yeah. This is Molly."

"You sick, Molly? Why your voice funny?"

"I'm at work, Xiaoming. This is a really, really bad place to talk."

"I know! What the hell you involved with?" he spat at me.

"And how is your day?" I replied.

"What you bring me? Why this model have the Earrings of Power?"

"Earring of what?"

"These supposed to be in elfin hoard," he replied.

"What?" I replied, ducking further behind the potted plant and looking right and left to make sure no one was listening in. "What did you say?" I hissed.

"These earrings. They were given to the elves and stored in hoard. They made by dwarfs. How did model get them?"

"I don't know," I replied. "I just stole them back."

"You, Molly Mackie, you in trouble."

"You think I don't know that?!" I replied. I paused as two grips walked by and gave them a little smile. As soon as they were out of hearing range I hissed into the phone. "I'm always in trouble."

"This time you in big trouble."

"Tell me something I don't know, Xiaoming," I replied.

"I will hold onto these."

"You sure about that?" I asked.

"You just lose them."

"No…" I replied. "I'll pick them up and bring them back to the Elfin Forest."

"If you found and you turned into a statue, we be in deep shit. If you bring back, elfin traitor just steal again. You will screw this up. I worked with you before. I will keep them so they don't get in bad hands again."

I sighed. There was a part of me that hated that I wasn't going to have a good excuse to hop over to see Killian. He was a pain in my ass, but I missed that guy. I wondered how the elves were doing. The fact I was getting mushy made me look sharply to see if there were any emotion vampires lurking around the corner, but it appeared these were just regular old feelings I was managing to have on my own.

"What else they have stolen over there?" Xiaoming yelled at me.

"I don't know! Jesus. I just found out about the earrings yesterday. And I brought them to you. And I'm in big trouble because I did."

"Bah. You in big trouble no matter what you do. You trouble magnet."

"Well, shall we avoid opening any further Pandora's boxes?"

"They have a Pandora box?!" he shouted.

"What? NO! That was just an expression of speech."

"You find out if they have a Pandora box!"

I sighed and slumped against the wall. "How the hell am I supposed to find out if they have a Pandora's box or anything else?"

"What are you, Molly?"

"A tracker."

"So, track magical object."

"A) I need to know what I'm looking for. B) I track people and monsters. I don't track objects."

"You track plenty objects."

"Not of my own free will!"

"You seem to be doing just fine."

"Don't bring that up," I replied.

"You put on your big girl pants and find thing to save world, Molly."

The line went dead. I leaned against the wall and sighed just as an incoming text chirped on the screen from Jeff. Cast needs a large caramel latte, two espresso shots, iced green tea with organic sugar, one medium black coffee. Not from commissary. Drive off lot to get them from Joey's Café. 1/2 hour away. Make sure hot gets here hot and ice in tea not melted. No petty cash. Will reimburse you through payroll next week. And get back to me on props ASAP.

Fuck my life.

CHAPTER EIGHTEEN

Coffee run hell survived, I walked into the prop house and flashed my badge at the bored, thirty-year-old hipster tending the desk. Without even glancing over the frames of his dark rimmed glasses, he held out a clipboard and a pencil to me. I took them and tried to give him my attempt at a smile. He was having none of that and just pushed his buds further into his canals.

"May you pop an eardrum," I muttered as I walked into the warehouse.

Room after room had been set up to show how nice some of the sets and prop pieces looked together. They were organized by era. Some were midcentury mod, some were midcentury medieval, and some were mid-post-apocalyptic century with no relevance to any trend at all besides "people are made of meat and everybody's gonna die." They probably made a bucketload renting out those props. Zombie flicks have such a following. I gotta say, though, it's all fun and games until you've actually lived through one.

But PTSD wasn't the thing that was causing my heart to go into palpitations. The room hummed with energy.

The hairs on my arms were standing on end. I brushed my hand against a table and got a zap. I had to try and pretend like the furniture didn't sting. I looked around and was just overwhelmed by the magic in the place. I mean, everyone has heard of movie magic, but I never thought they actually meant movie MAGIC.

Is that why this lousy studio had managed to make one blockbuster after the next? It didn't really have anything to do with story or characters or plot or writing or direction or technical prowess, it was that they were filming magical objects and casting the entire globe under a hypnotic trance? If they already wielded this kind of power, what were they going to do if they got a hold of elfin glamour?

I pretended like I was super interested in a vase that looked like it had been raided from some Scottish castle. The arc of magic actually jumped across space to boop me on the nose.

"How the hell did they manage to get you?" I whispered.

"Talking to oneself is a sign of insanity," came a voice.

Fucking Graham. I turned around and there he was.

"Just noticing how beautiful this is," I replied, trying to put a chipper chirp into my voice. I didn't want any negative feelings feeding into anything in this room. I felt like I was wandering through a pitch-dark dynamite warehouse with a flippin' match to light the way. "It looks like it is a real antique."

He stood so close to me that I could smell the leather of his stupid duster. "It is," he replied. "You wanna tell me what you figured out about this cesspool and I'll tell you what I've figured out?"

I glared at Graham. The guy was an ass. I was 100% sure he was going to double-cross me. But those words he said earlier rang in my mind. He was an enemy of my enemy, which made him my frienemy, too. My life and Killian's life, in addition to the existence of the entire human race, depended on me figuring out what was sucking all the energy into the studio and stopping it. And dollars to doughnuts, something here was at the heart of it.

"You go first," I said.

Graham reached over and started fiddling with a letter opener. I took it out of his hand, ignoring the psychic punch it gave me, and set it back down on the desk.

"What?" he said, a little insulted.

"You have no idea what that will do."

"Oh, actually, I do." He grabbed the letter opener, stuck it into thin air, and that sucker cut through the dimensions.

"What the hell?!" I yanked it out of the veil and healed up the rift, and then proceeded to bend the letter opener just enough to render it useless. "They had this thing just lying around here?!"

"They are all just lying around here, Maggie," said Graham. "Guess what? The founder of this studio? Mr. Firebrand himself? He was insistent they use actual antique props and vintage costume pieces in all his movies. He's been collecting stuff since before movies could talk. And then the tradition has been carried on, people say, because of all the HD televisions and how you can see everything. But THAT's the biggest load of crap anyone's ever tried to shovel at me."

"He has a point," I replied thinking of some plastic surgery I'd seen that made the case for returning to the world of standard definition.

Graham wasn't buying it. "He's a hoarder."

"Could he have been an elf?" I asked. "Just gathering up stuff that maybe his people lost?"

"How should I know?" said Graham, like I was dumb for piping up. "All I know is he went around buying antiques. And then the folks who took over for him after he keeled over went around buying antiques. I mean, there's antiques here that have absolutely no relevance to any movie that has ever been green lit. No value whatsoever except they all seem to have an extra little bit of sparkle."

"So he is a hoarder. They are creating their own hoard," I replied, looking around the prop warehouse with a little bit of admiration for the ingenuity. "No one would think to come here. Security is almost as tight as having a dragon."

"Bingo," said Graham. "And it seems like this was all working out well until this takeover. Now that these Shareholders are in the picture and that creepy CEO with the eye shine, I hear the current vice president is crying himself to sleep every night like a little bitch."

"Everyone cries."

"I don't cry."

"That's because you're an asshole," I pointed out.

"Touché," he replied. He crossed his arms and widened his stance like he was getting ready for me to tackle him with information. "Okay. Now you tell me what you've found out."

I rubbed the bottom of my lip with my forefinger. I so didn't want to tell him anything.

"I see that look, Maggie," warned Graham. "I know that look. I showed you. Your turn to show me. If shit's going down, I need a little heads up to get the hell out of here."

I sighed. I hated the guy, but he A) hadn't ratted me out and B) had given me some sort of useful information. "There's some jewelry that went missing," I said, leaving out the part that I was the reason the jewelry went missing.

"You stole it, didn't you?" he guessed with a smirk.

"Stop it!" I said, smacking his arm, but also not confirming his guess.

"You totally stole it. What? That elf of yours didn't get you a Valentine's present?"

"We're. Not. Dating," I heaved.

"Whatever."

"Do you want this info or not?" I replied.

Graham shrugged.

"They're elfin."

Graham gave another shrug. "So, they're stealing from elves, too. Or buying something that someone stole from the elves?"

"The elves didn't know it was missing," I replied.

"Oh," he said, his eyes suddenly twinkling with this juicy bit of gossip. "Oh, so there's someone on the inside."

"Bingo."

"Interesting…" he said. "Huh. Wonder who that might be…"

"Well, if you think of anyone, let me know, will you? So that I can kill him?"

"Might be a 'her'."

"I'm pretty sure it's a 'him'."

"Why? You sexist or something? Why's it always gotta be a guy?"

"Because, thus far, all the douche bags I've run into have had dicks."

"Chicks are dicks, too."

"Shut up, Graham."

"Well, maybe some dick with a vagina is pissed that the queen got to be the prettiest, prettiest princess for all these eons and she decided it was high time for her to get some of this good shit."

"Why would you think that?"

He smacked his forehead ironically. "Think, Maggie. Guys? They're gonna go for the swords and fucking maces. Chicks? Only a chick would pick out a pair of earrings to steal."

"They're easier to carry and smuggle away," I replied, pointing out the total logic.

"What the hell is a dude gonna do with a pair of fucking earrings? We don't even have holes in our ears in order to wear that sort of shit."

"That is a gross overgeneralization," I stated. "In lots of cultures—"

"Blah blah blah," he cut me off. "It was a chick."

"Put your money where your mouth is," I challenged.

"What the fuck have you got that I could possibly want?"

I thought for a second. "If it's a 'chick', I'll do your coffee run."

He smiled. "Now you're talkin'. That's, like, better than getting a favor from an elf."

"And you take mine if it's a dude."

He held out his hand. "You got yourself a bet."

"A bet you're going to lose."

"Sucker."

He looked down my shirt.

"Excuse me, but did you just look down my shirt?" I asked.

"Don't flatter yourself." He pointed at the stack of papers in my hands. "I was reading over your chest. It's like reading over someone's shoulder, but with a moderately better view."

"I hate you so much."

"The feeling is mutual. What's that in your hand?"

"I need to find out when these props are going to be delivered," I replied.

"Psssh... that's easy." He shouted over at the counter. "Mason! When the fuck are you going to deliver the props to Soundstage 13?"

Mason, which I guess was his name, took his ear buds out and glanced at his spreadsheet. "Friday."

"Poker tomorrow night?" Graham asked, giving him a thumbs-up.

Mason shrugged and then put his ear buds back in.

"Fucker," said Graham.

"Thanks for finding that out for me," I replied.

He slung his arm across my shoulder. "Listen, Maggie, Hollywood is a boys club and you, being a girl, are not invited."

"I was, seriously, just trying to express my gratitude and

you had to go ruin it, Graham."

"It's what I do."

I picked his fingers off my shoulder and dropped his hand away from me. "Touch me again and I will break your fucking wings."

He swaggered away, completely unfazed, shooting finger guns at some other P.A. "Jooohnnny!"

I saw Johnny roll his eyes as soon as Graham walked past. Glad to know I wasn't the only one. I probably should have told Graham about the emotion vampires, but figured if they were looking for depth of feeling, they'd find themselves starving around him.

I headed in the direction of what I thought was the front door, but got turned around. There was too much magic. I found myself in a maze of desks and bookcases and bars and then went through a doorway and found myself in the garden patio section of the prop house.

I had to steady myself on the doorframe. "Oh."

Amidst the fake trees and fake box hedges, there were rows and rows of marble statues, and I recognized them all. They were all World Walkers. Every last one of them. Portal maker after portal maker, one right beside the next. Some looked like they were screaming. Some looked like they were caught waking up.

I felt someone stand next to me. "Creepy, huh?" said Johnny, the guy Graham had just made finger guns at. "We used to have more of them, but there was a mix-up in one of the communications and they ended up blowing up a bunch of them."

"They blew them up?" I asked, my mouth dry.

"Yeah. Sucks because, you know, they were really old and valuable and stuff. But they were insured, so it's fine. Besides, they caught it on film and evidently it looks badass. Heard they're already putting together a montage of slo-mo footage where you can see them just ripping apart. You feeling okay?" Johnny asked. "You got super pale like you saw a ghost or something. Like, you-should-get-a-spray-tan pale."

Now, I have seen a ghost and this is not how I look like when I see a ghost. I looked like a woman who found out the people she worked with had been transformed into marble statues by a medusa and then had been blown up in a mass execution and realized that she could have been one of them.

"I'm just feeling a little woozie," I replied.

"Juice cleanse, am I right?" he asked, like I had just revealed some big secret we now shared together. "Don't worry. Just get through to day three and when you get rid of all that bloating you've got going on around your stomach area? You are going to be so glad you did it."

I so needed him to shut up right now. "Any chance they have a bottle of water around this place?"

Johnny handed me his tablet. "On it. I'll be right back." He stopped halfway out of the room. "Oh! Do you want still? Sparkling? Ice? No ice? Any particular aquifer?"

"Just water," I replied.

I watched him leave and then slumped down into a white, ironwork chair. I looked at the frozen forms of all my ex-friends and ex-rivals and ex-coworkers. "I'll free you guys," I promised. "Somehow I'll free you."

CHAPTER NINETEEN

I pulled up into the park lot. I was about an hour-and-a-half northwest of Los Angeles near a small airport in Camarillo. There was a big factory outlet and some strip malls near the freeway, but beyond that bit of civilization, it was mostly rolling farmlands and California hills. I hoped I was far enough away that if the forces of darkness traced my call, they wouldn't be able to pinpoint where I was actually living. I apologized to the little private four-seater airplanes if any vampires showed up looking for Frequent Biter miles.

I jogged over to a pay phone and dialed Killian's number.

"Greetings this eventide?" came his confused voice.

"Don't say who this is," I cautioned.

"MA-- my maiden warrior…?" he replied.

"Maiden might be a bit of a stretch."

I heard him chuckle on the other line. A chuckle that broke into a cough. Elves don't get sick. Not unless their queen is dying. But he tried to joke anyway, "Thou doth protest too much."

I bonked my head on the metal pay phone hood in

frustration. I needed to figure out how the hell to free her. But I had this favor hanging over my head and, like they say in a crash, you gotta put your oxygen mask on first. At least I could help him a little with his. "Listen, you have a traitor in your midst."

"I have assumed this was the case."

"Someone with access to the elfin hoards."

Killian didn't speak for a little while.

"Are you there?" I asked.

"I am!" he replied. "I am pondering which member of our tribe would most likely be the villainous perpetrator of this offense…"

"In plainspeak, elf."

"I am 'figuring out whodunit.'"

"Thanks, elf." I sat there for a moment cradling the receiver and decided to give him a hard time. "You're spending so much time in that forest, I could barely figure out what you were saying."

"Well, someone, who shall remain nameless in this accusation, abandoned me to a mission of the utmost importance with little to no ancillary support."

"I miss you, too."

"And I, you. Are you having any forward movement on your quest?"

Fucking "quest". I needed to get this wrapped up and the elf out of the forest before he forgot how to have a normal conversation.

"There's a new breed of vampires," I said, looking around as if just speaking the word 'vampire' would alert them to my presence. "They feed off emotions."

"Ah! So you are spending your days mastering the art of emotional control?"

"Don't be ridiculous."

"So you are not."

"I am too busy making coffee runs."

"I do not understand your meaning. Are you running with coffee or is this some human euphemism for bowel distress?"

I laughed. "I am running with coffee to people who are in distress."

"It sounds as if you have taken over my role in our partnership."

"Pretty much."

We sat there in silence for a little while longer. I finally piped up with, "I discovered these earrings that were supposed to be in the elfin hoard. Earrings of Power. That's how we figured out it was an inside job."

"Who is 'we'?"

"Xiaoming and I."

"Ah! You are assembling our band of warriors!"

"Sure," I replied, not mentioning I hadn't broached that subject with Xiaoming at all. I doubt I could get him to leave his living room, much less meet up on a weekly basis to save the world. "And then we discovered there is this warehouse filled with magical treasures."

"I am glad Xiaoming has been of assistance."

"Oh," I said, pausing awkwardly. "No. Not Xiaoming. Graham. Graham and I. We discovered a warehouse with a magical hoard on the studio lot."

Now there was a silence on the line that had absolutely nothing to do with silence. "You are… partnering with… Graham? The bounty hunter? The one that betrayed you and is responsible for my queen being in a state of thrall?"

"No."

"Please expound, Maggie."

My blood ran cold. "You just said my name."

"I am sorry. I am so sorry," Killian replied, panicking.

"I have to go."

"I know. I miss you."

"I miss you, too. I have to go before they trace this."

"Godspeed."

"I'll be in touch."

"Do not trust Graham."

"I don't." And then I hung up. I scanned the parking

lot as I ran to my car. Fuckity fuck. Why did Killian have to say my name? I had no idea how long I had. Five minutes? Ten? A minute? If his phone was tapped, they could be here any second.

I opened my door and turned on my engine. I peeled out as quickly as I could without calling attention to myself. I kept checking my rearview mirror. It had been a mistake to call Killian. It had been a mistake not to reach out to him through the established channels.

But fuck it.

I smiled.

It was worth it.

CHAPTER TWENTY

I pulled into my apartment complex. The lights were blazing in my windows. I wondered what Pipistrelle had gotten up to today. I hauled my tired ass up the six flights of stairs to the third floor and opened my door. The entire place was 100% completely furnished. I mean, we're talking sofas, end tables, dining room sets. It was an Swedish wonderland of pre-fab furniture. Unfortunately, Pipistrelle had mistaken me for a small child, because he had decided to err on the more junior side of stylings. There was a television, but fitted into a rounded, cartoony looking wardrobe. There were small, foam armchairs more Pipistrelle-sized than Maggie-sized. There was a carpet on the floor that looked like a city street, which would have been great if I were a preschooler still playing with fire trucks and Matchbox cars. There was a four-foot-tall circus play tent in the corner. I just hoped he had picked that for himself as opposed to thinking that's where I would be hanging out. The window coverings were a pinecone and hedgehog print. The side tables looked like overgrown mushrooms.

"Surprise!" he squeaked, arms overhead like presenting

a showcase on the Price-Is-Right.

"Wow, Pipistrelle," I remarked through a forced smile. "You outdid yourself."

"Hip hip hooray! The Mighty Tracker Maggie appreciates her new apartment!"

"Appreciate doesn't even come close," I said. "Soooo... tell me all about your decorating decisions."

"Well," he said, clasping his hands together and curling his shoulders like he was about to confide in me a delicious secret. "We are now roommates and so I decided to get things you and I and Killian of Greenwold would delight in."

"How... delightful!" I replied. "But... um... where should I put my guns?"

He marched right over to the small hall closet and opened it up. He had organized all sorts of weaponry into sealed totes stacked evenly on chrome shelving. I don't even know where he GOT all those weapons. I'm pretty sure they weren't in the catalog. It was pretty darn sweet.

"I thought this was the part that YOU would like," he announced in his squeaky little voice.

"You guessed right," I said, dropping my coat on a dining room chair. "You have got a knack for this organizational thing, haven't you?"

He picked it up, dusted it off, climbed up the shelving, and hung it for me. I sighed, realizing I was going to have to be on my best behavior.

He jumped off the shelf and ran over to the circus tent. "I have made myself my own apartment," he informed me, holding back the red fabric door flap.

And, really, how could you be mad at the guy. He obviously had given it all a lot of thought. Killian would like the woodsy stuff. Pipistrelle seemed to like the circus stuff. And I didn't like anything except the arsenal of weaponry, so he had met that requirement, too.

I knelt down and looked inside. It was covered in balls of yarn and craft supplies. "Wow."

"When I have some free time, I shall make some doily wards for your home to keep the vampires away, Maggie."

"Ah!" I said, realizing I needed to cut this off at the pass. "Pipistrelle, actually, I really need you to come into work with me tomorrow. Really, really. There is big trouble and I sure could use some help."

He looked around the apartment with worried eyes. "But I have not completed the haven for the Mighty Maggie yet..."

"It's okay! We need to save the world! Jobs are good! They let us buy things!" I followed his line of sight and a thought suddenly occurred to me. "Pipistrelle?"

"Mmmm-hmmm?"

"How did you buy all of this?"

"AH!" he said with joy. "There is a plastic rectangle called a 'card' and you give it to the people and they give you the things!"

"Oh, no." I said. "You are done. This haven is most definitely done."

CHAPTER TWENTY-ONE

I pulled into the parking garage and turned off the car. Pipistrelle was strapped into the seat beside me. I probably needed to get him a booster seat.

"Okay, Pipistrelle," I said, ready to outline my plan for getting him in. "I've got to go over to Soundstage 13." I reached into my backseat and brought out my backpack. "I was thinking I could put you in my bag and carry you in—"

Pipistrelle held up one of his little hands and looked at me like I was an amateur. "Do not fret, Maggie MacKay. I shall get there without your assistance."

And with no further ado, he unclicked his seat belt, climbed out the front door, and was off like a rocket. By the time I unbuckled and looked out the deck, he was weaving his way between oncoming cars, crossing the street like a toddler on a skateboard.

"If you get yourself squished..." I muttered at him as I watched him go. But he made it across and then disappeared into the hedge.

I, meanwhile, crossed the street according to the crosswalk signals, waited in line behind all the other plebs, and finally made it to the front of the line at the guard shack.

"First day here?" the guard asked with an excessively welcome smile.

"No," I replied as he looked through my bag. "You see me every day. Like, everyday."

"Have a great day!" he said with a salute.

By the time I got to the soundstage, it had been like twenty minutes. Pipistrelle was sitting in the driver's seat of a golf cart and was making racing noises.

"Pipistrelle!" I said, hiding him with my jacket. "People can't see you!"

"Oh! They already saw me," he said with a beaming grin. "I am in disguise. I am the misshapen child of one of the directors!"

"That's... really... not PC..." I awkwardly pointed out.

"They are all mightily impressed by the opportunities the studio is providing to a brave child facing the challenging circumstances that I am!" he parroted.

"You couldn't have come up with some other explanation?" I said, feeling really uncomfortable by the way women were walking by, placing their hands on their hearts and giving Pipistrelle sympathetic yet supportive glances.

"They are going to raise money for me in a walk-a-thon!"

"Okay, Pipistrelle," I said, stopping him before things went too far. I mean, farther than the too far they had already gone to. "The reason why I need you to hide is because there are a lot of vampires and monsters and Other Siders here who know you are not a misshapen child."

"Oh," he said, suddenly whispering.

"If anyone asks, do you have a work permit to remain on Earth?"

"YES!" he shouted. "THANKS TO MAGG—"

I put my hand over his wide mouth. "I need you to

leave out that last part. The part where you say my name. Right?" He shook his head in agreement and I removed my hand. My phone started buzzing and I pulled it out of my pocket. "Crap."

"What excrement finds itself upon your phone?" he asked, pulling out a handkerchief to hand to me.

"Not excrement," I replied, showing him the screen. "Just a bunch of people wanting coffee and expecting me to front the cost out of my own pocket until payroll can pay me back in two weeks."

He grabbed my phone and began scanning the text messages. He handed it back. "Leave it to me!"

He beeped the horn of the golf cart and was off like a rocket. I have no idea where he was planning on going in that cart, but I knew for a fact people were going to be grumpy if he thought he could just bring them coffee from the commissary. I was going to have to re-add "coffee run" to my to-do list. I turned and walked into the soundstage.

Jeff was sitting there rubbing his eyebrows as two stern men dressed like police officers walked away. I was praying they were extras. I was pretty sure they were not. I walked over and gave Jeff a little wave.

"What's going on?" I asked.

"You pissed off someone important," he replied under his breath as he watched the guards go.

"What the hell?!" I said. "I do the job that people ask me to do."

Jeff glanced around and pulled me into his office with a conspiratorial look. He shut the door behind us and turned the volume down on his walkie-talkie. "Turns out that Ms. D'rela stole those earrings from the costume department, because costume department had also filed a report that they were missing. And then either you or the housekeeping staff, not knowing that her hotel room had been burgled, cleaned everything up, which means that there are no fingerprints anywhere, which means, as the only person folks can fire, now everyone is pissed off at you."

"I DIDN'T DO ANYTHING!"

"Shit flows downhill, Maggie."

"I don't think that's the real saying."

"You're going to be the fall person on this," he said, poking me on the shoulder, "which means you're going to get your ass canned, which means I'm going to end up dead, which means you're going to end up dead."

"This is nuts."

"Can you remember anything… anything at all? I need you to tell me the truth."

I shrugged, sticking to the lie I'd been spinning all this time. "I just went into her hotel room and packed her stuff. I didn't see any jewelry."

"Those were about $200,000 worth of diamonds."

My jaw dropped. "How much?"

"Two-zero-zero-comma-zero-zero-zero."

"She definitely should have put them into the house safe."

"Our costume department shouldn't have let them out of their sight," said Jeff, looking like he was barely keeping his shit together. "They are irreplaceable antiques. Belonged to some Russian queen or something."

"In light of their value, why did the costume department let them out of their sight?"

"Well, that's the thing. They received earrings back, they were just facsimiles. Great facsimiles."

"Oh."

"Yep. Ms. D'rela says that she returned them, but she is no diamond expert and was not able to tell the difference between what she wore and what she handed in."

I squinted at him in mock thoughtfulness. "Yet her agent yelled at us about missing earrings. Earrings that would not have been reported as missing or even in her hotel room if she had returned them."

"Yep."

"Idiot."

"Yep."

I couldn't help chuckling and Jeff joined me. "I mean, COME ON. If you're going to lie, you have to be able to keep your lies straight…"

"It's hard for some people to remember what they're supposed to say when the words haven't been written down for them."

"So, how is she explaining it to the police?" I asked, jerking my thumb back towards the guys who had just left.

"Evidently, not well."

"Huh?"

"They're hauling her in for theft."

"Oooo… that is not going to look good in the tabloids…"

"You're pretty new to this industry, aren't you?" commented Jeff with a sardonic laugh. "If you're broke like her and got a cocaine habit that shoves all the dollars you make up your sinus cavities, it's a GREAT way to make sure your name stays at the top of people's minds. All press is good press. There's nothing that can't be made better by a stint in rehab and a round of talk shows to admire her bravery."

"Wait. So… this was like… a publicity stunt?"

He put one finger on his nose and pointed the other at me. "You betcha."

This little jerk had been planning to play the studio like a fiddle. Unfortunately, now that she had been caught, she was probably going through some emotional angst, which meant she was feeding the vampires here, which means I had managed to do their job for them. But Jeff didn't know all the thoughts rambling through my mind. He just suddenly saw me get really quiet and thoughtful.

He leaned in towards me, hazarding a completely incorrect guess as to which wheels were spinning in my head. "And yes, this movie's going to be delayed due to reshoots, which means you're STILL getting canned."

"For what?"

"For breathing in the wrong place. Tell me what actually happened, Maggie, so I can help you."

I shook my head and held up my hands. "Nothing. Absolutely nothing happened. It all went down exactly as I told you."

"Do you swear on your old partner's dead body."

"He's not dead," I pointed out.

Jeff gave me a look.

"He's not."

"Would you bet a favor on it?"

"I don't utter those words even in jest," I replied.

There was a banging on the door, which cut our conversation mercifully short. Chaz came wandering into the office sipping what looked like a cup of coffee.

"Great job with the coffee, Maggie," he said, taking off his sunglasses and perching them backwards on his head. "FINALLY. You were, seriously, the worst. I'll make sure you get paid back." He turned to Jeff. "Reimburse her once she provides a receipt, would you? But make sure she has a receipt. Also, I need you, Jeff. Chop! Chop!" He snapped his fingers at Jeff and walked away.

Jeff looked so utterly resigned to the whole thing as he gathered up his papers and began walking towards the door. But he paused for a moment to give me a second look as he put two and two together. "How did you get coffee when you were sitting right here with me the whole time?"

I wiggled my fingers and gave him a winning smile. "Magic."

CHAPTER TWENTY-TWO

I pulled my car around to the rear of the church sanctuary and chewed on my bottom lip. I didn't understand why, with aaaalll the security in place to keep my whereabouts a secret, Father Killarney would choose to have me meet with him here at his parish. Seemed like an easy place to stake out. But then again, maybe nobody cared. I mean, truth be told, no one had come looking for me. I hadn't had any brushups with the authorities. Maybe I was thinking I was a bigger shot than I actually was. In fact, I was getting a little offended that I hadn't even been attacked by a vampire—not even once—since I skipped out on the Other Side. I had no idea what gave, but if I had ditched my family and my partner and set my house on fire for no reason, I was going to be highly irate.

The light to the rectory was still lit and I saw Father Killian's silhouette walk to the window, look out, and then disappear again. Figured he was probably looking for me, and that meant I should probably get inside before he called my parents to tell them I was missing.

I stepped out of my car and walked up to the door. I knocked lightly. The door opened and Father Killarney stood there looking at me.

"Hey!" I said. "Can I come in?"

"I don't know, Maggie-girl. Can you?" he asked in his lilting Irish brogue.

"What?" I asked.

And then he took a glass bowl from behind his back, dipped his hand into the water and shook the droplets onto my face.

"What the hell—" I said, wiping the water from my eyes and stepping inside.

He grabbed me by the arm. "Not a vampire." He then pulled out a flashlight and shone it in my pupils. I squinted and pulled away. "No doppelganger eye shine." He then sniffed my general direction. "And no ghoul decay." He shut the door, put down the bowl, wrapped me up in an embrace, and grinned broadly. "It's you! Ah, Maggie-girl! I have been missing you mightily! What have you been up to?"

I pulled away from him, and his unshaved whiskers got caught in my hair. "Forgive me if I repeat myself, but what the hell?"

He pointed up at the ceiling. "You're in a house of God now, you are. Don't go speaking the words that should not be spoken under this roof."

"You host an illicit poker game here every Wednesday night," I replied as I followed him into the conference room where the church council meetings are supposed to take place. "I think I'm okay."

The room was white plaster. Lining the walls were light oak bookcases filled with bibles and theology tomes. The conference table matched the wood of the cases and the chairs matched the table. Their seats were covered in a coarsely woven, red, industrial-looking material that went out of style in the late 80s.

"Your mother and father have been terribly worried about you. How are you doing in this new life you've created?" he asked going over to a mini-fridge to pull out the bottle of sacramental wine and pour me a cup.

"I'm certainly learning patience and humility," I said, taking the glass from him.

He sat down at the long, wooden table and I joined him. "So, what is it that is worth coming out of hiding to see me for?"

I took a sip of the sweet wine and grimaced. It tasted like fermented prune juice. "Ugh. You serve this to people?"

"Bottle is getting a bit old," said Father Killarney, toasting me with his glass. "Got to finish it up."

"You're on your own," I replied, pushing it away from me. "So, turns out, the vampires have evolved."

Father Killarney emptied his glass and poured himself another like he was going to need a little help getting through this new news. "Evolved you say?"

"We've got the regular bloodsucking vampires that you and I know and love. But this new breed sucks out emotions. They cause longing and depression and despair."

"How interesting," he said, stroking his stubbly chin. He leaned back in his seat and I knew I was in for it. I got comfortable as he started rambling on. "Did you know, Maggie, that when you go back to the original Greek word for 'sin', there is no morality attached to it. It just means 'going the wrong direction.' It carries no more weight than taking a left instead of a right. But when we talk about the seven deadly sins, the seven wrong directions that will kill you, despair is weighted the most. More than gluttony or envy or rage... despair is the one that will kill you the fastest."

I did not know this. "And that's what these vampires are doing. They love this negative shit."

Father Killarney glared at me like a disappointed parent.

"'Cussing' is nowhere on the seven deadly wrong directions list," I pointed out.

"I'll have to do a little research on that before I let you go speaking those words under my roof."

I rolled my eyes and rephrased my statement. "These vampires are doing things to stir up these negative emotions, and then they are feasting on it."

"Interesting," said Father Killarney. "So what do you wish to do about it?"

"Um…" I was at a loss. "Not feel a negative emotion again for as long as I live?"

"What is your Plan B?"

"I dunno. Don't you, with all of your spiritual whateverness, have a cure for the blues?"

"Well, there's prayer and meditation—"

"I mean something that works."

He shook his head and pointed his finger at me. "Don't go knocking it until you've tried it, Maggie-girl."

"I need to know how to defeat these bastards," I said, "not think them to death. Do I poke 'em through the heart or chop off their heads or set them on fire or what?"

"I'll look that up for you," he said as he poured himself another glass. "And if you get some of those negative feelings, just imagine a river, and your thought is just a little leaf floating on the water, and watch it sail past."

"I'll keep that in mind the next time I've got a vampire aiming for my throat."

"Makes you long for the good old days when vampwolves and werepires were all you had to worry about, doesn't it?" he laughed with a wistful sigh.

"Yep. Speaking of which, Father Killarney. Not that I'm complaining or anything, but I have not heard hide-nor-hair from a single vampwolf or werepire since I got here. What gives?"

He scratched his unshaved cheek. "Maybe each side is just glad to have you do their dirty work."

"Meaning?"

"Every vampire, bloodsucker or otherwise, that you kill means one they don't have to. You're doing their dirty work, which makes you valuable."

I dipped my finger into my wine and traced the rim of my glass slowly. "There's another thing…" I said, my voice trailing off.

"What is it?"

"I ran into Graham…"

Father Killarney sat forward in his seat in alarm. "That bastard? Where's he at? I'll kill 'em."

Seems the sacramental wine was filling him with a bit too much spirit for a man his age. I pushed Father Killarney back. "It's okay. He busted out of prison and he's in hiding at the same place I'm hiding. We're frienemies right now."

Father Killarney looked like he was biting back some very choice words but let me continue.

"He said that there was a prophecy," I mentioned casually. "Said something about how I was destined to bring down the vampires and that's why they are always gunning for me. Is there… is there anything you've been meaning to tell me that you just never got around to?"

"Ah," he said, tucking his chin down to his chest in what I could only imagine was uncomfortable embarrassment. "That."

"So you DO know something," I replied, crossing my arms. "I can't believe you didn't tell me!"

"I didn't know if it was you or your sister! Or your mother," he explained.

"I'm the only one who goes around killing vampires!"

"When it comes to prophecies, even the smallest of stones can shake the grandest of mountains!"

"Speak it!" I demanded, pointing my finger at him. "Tell me what exactly I'm in for."

"SOMEONE," Father Killarney corrected me, "Not necessarily you, but someone in your family is destined to bring down the vampires. It is one of the reasons your uncle was so dead-set against your father marrying your mother."

"What?"

"The prophecy says there is a woman from your line who will take them down."

"I need the words, Father Killarney," I said, collapsing my head into my arms. "I need the exact words."

"Well, how should I know? It is been years since I looked at it," he replied with exasperation at my dramatics. "You think I go walking around memorizing pieces of ancient prophecy to be pulled out whenever someone asks for it? I gave you the general gist. I'm not the Internet."

"Would the Internet have it?" I asked with some hope.

He shrugged. "You could look it up."

"I'll do that."

"Let me know what you find."

"Fine."

He took another sip from his glass and I decided to rethink my position on this lousy wine. I grabbed my glass and gulped half of it down to do the job, then pulled out my cell phone. I Googled "ancient prophecy mackay vampire" but only came up with your standard malware and penis enlargement sites. I threw my phone back down.

I folded my arms and glared at Father Killarney. "Well, could you look it up for me when you get a chance?" I asked.

He shrugged. "If I get a chance."

"What's with the Xiaoming-like resistance? You going to pick up smoking and making my life miserable?"

"Maybe you're not supposed to know what's in the prophecy."

"Am I supposed to not know what is in the prophecy?"

"Maybe."

"That doesn't answer the question!"

"If I told you, then maybe I would be breaking the prophecy. Or causing the prophecy to happen. It is hard to know with prophecies. They don't come with assembly instructions. They just sort of mention things might happen in such a way that they seem almost applicable to any situation."

"Are you saying that my prophecy is about as detailed as a Sunday Times horoscope?"

"I'm just cautioning that perhaps you should trust the people who care about you more than some fallen angel who may or may not have a bone to pick with you."

I sighed. Prophecy. No prophecy. He was right. I should have learned the last time I tangled with Graham not to trust him as far as I could throw him. Father Killarney seemed to see my acceptance of the situation.

He reached out and patted the back of my hand. "The emotions and thoughts you are feeling are just a leaf on the water, floating by."

"I'm supposed to be able to defeat these emo-vamps with THAT?"

He shrugged. "That or Valium."

"I'm going to skip the Valium."

"Excellent choice." He took another sip from his glass. "So, you found out about the new vampires. You found out about a prophecy you didn't need to know about. What else have you discovered, Maggie?"

"That I hate the film and television industry."

CHAPTER TWENTY-THREE

I got to work a couple days later and the lot was abuzz with something. I mean, everyone was walking fast and working hard and on high alert. I got into the soundstage. There was a scrawny looking woman the size of an eight-year-old child standing next to Craft Services, chewing miserably on a stick of celery.

I went over and grabbed a bagel, smearing it with a mountain of cream cheese.

"Bread will make you fat," she said, looking at my choice like I had stacked sardines on top of an Oreo.

"I can use the calories," I said, taking a huge bite. The cheese left a line across my cheeks. "Why so serious?"

She wiped away the tears that spilled out of her eyes. "This show has been a nightmare."

"Maybe you're just hungry," I replied, offering her the plastic tub of red licorice ropes.

She waved it away in a distracted manner. "That won't make it better."

"Um… imagine your feelings like a leaf on the river just floating by…?" I offered. I really sucked at this cheering-up business.

But it seemed to do something for her. She smiled and nodded, like I had just spoken the most profound words she had ever heard. "Yeah. You're right! We're all just temporary. Nothing lasts forever. I should keep in mind that this too shall pass. Namaste."

"Um… you're welcome?" I took a Twizzler for myself.

"What's your name?"

I caught myself before I said the wrong name. "Molly. I'm a P.A. I've been on your set. For weeks now."

"I'm sure I won't remember you, so don't be offended if I ask again," she replied. "It is just SO hard to remember names. Or faces."

"Ditto," I answered back. She didn't seem as cool with my response as I was with hers. I motioned to the outside world with my floppy licorice. "So, what's going on today?"

"Oh, they're gearing up for the big release," she replied with a shrug.

"Big release?"

"Do you live under a rock?"

I smiled through a stiff smile. "Pretty much."

"The big reboot of Legions of Space opens today. I heard it is TOTALLY on fleek."

"Oh," I said, pretending like I understood anything that she was talking about. "I never really caught the first one."

"Oh, me neither," she replied. "It is SO old. It came out in like… what… 1984? That's like… before the turn of the century. SO long ago."

I smiled my angelic smile and thought of that goddamned fucking leaf on the fucking river.

She rattled on. "But it has this huge cult following and they are massively excited about it coming back. I even saw some of the original cast here on the lot. I hear they did some cameos and stuff, but if you ask me, they got really old."

"Well, it has been… what… thirty years since the first one came out?"

She flicked back her perfectly curled, sun-kissed hair. "I just think if you're going to do a reboot, you could at least find people who know to bleach their teeth."

I hid my teeth behind my lips. "Mmmm…"

"Although I heard a bunch of them die in this movie, so maybe it was like… this artistic statement about death where they were like.. embracing what happens to people when they turn forty."

"Um… forty is the new thirty," I pointed out.

"Only if you're Oprah," she informed me. "So, anyways, they're doing this big release to all the digital theaters across the globe at one time and then doing a big press announcement. It's a TOTALLY big deal."

"Trudy!" We both turned and the big-boobed, blonde-haired costumer came striding over. "You're needed on set."

Trudy snapped to attention and offered me her half-eaten celery. "Want this? I am stuffed. I hate to let it go to waste."

"Oh, it's okay," I replied. "I'm full."

"I know," she replied. "You ate SO much." She nodded in sympathy and patted my belly before walking away. I had no idea how to even react. But then she turned back to me. "Oh! And by the way, you are getting SO much better on the coffee runs. Really stepping up on the job. You should be proud. You know, I have a feeling one of these days, you'll be more than just a P.A. I can really see you being… like… whatever comes after P.A. Like, a vice P.A. or something? You totally have the potential to be that. Just keep dreaming and reaching for the stars. Like a leaf."

Trudy flicked her hair over her shoulder and smiled, looking like she had just spread a little needed sunshine out into the world.

The costumer put her arm around Trudy's shoulder and hustled her away. I overheard her say to Trudy, "Was that woman making you feel uncomfortable?" And then she looked over her shoulder at me with wary disgust.

To which I could hear Trudy insist, "No, she was nice... I mean, she's fat, but she's nice..." before fading away behind the flats.

I felt Jeff walk up behind me. "Bread will make you fat."

"Shut up, Jeff."

"You know what won't make you fat?"

"What?"

"Making our director his smoothie."

I groaned. Jeff gave me a shove in the direction of the trailer. "And make sure it is nice and smooth! He said he had the worst gas pains EVER on set yesterday. And today he has to get over to the amusement park for the big screening and the press announcement and farting in the middle of that would not look good for the studio. He wanted you to know that. Specifically. Farting would not be good for the press."

"Tell him thanks for the additional clarification."

"His gastrointestinal wellness is in your hands."

"Got it."

"And after you're done, I have an EXTRA special treat for you."

It did not take a psychic to understand what was in store was not anything I wanted to be involved with.

CHAPTER TWENTY-FOUR

I delegated smoothie-making to Pipistrelle, who was so excited by the prospects of a whole blender all to himself, I felt bad I hadn't offered it to him before. I also managed to pass along the compliments on his coffee runs, so he let me in on a little secret.

"I have purchased an espresso maker and have made all of their coffee by myself!" he announced, showing me the broom closet where he had set himself up as a barista.

I so didn't even want to see the credit card bill when it came in. "Just save me the receipt..." I replied, softly closing the door and walking away. I guess I was now the proud owner of an espresso machine. All I needed was to build a house around it. Although from the look of the thing, it very well could have been the price of a house.

But the speed at which I supposedly blended Chaz his smoothie seemed to cheer Jeff up. Gotta feel terrible for a guy whose bright spot is a P.A. who can work a blender. Not that I could actually work a blender. But hypothetically speaking.

He sent me down into the administrative file rooms to collate script rewrites. I'm guessing Trudy wasn't too pleased with her new words, because I could hear her wailing from all the way across the soundstage.

I sat in the dim, windowless room surrounded by stacks of paperwork. I felt like my eyeballs were so dry, they were going to fall out of my head. Give me a monster bite anytime, my hands were covered in paper cuts and my nails were tearing off down near the cuticles. I thought I was going to lose my mind.

The pink pages needed to replace the yellow pages in the blue script. Although now I wondered if it was the yellow pages that needed to stay and the blue pages that needed to go. It was all just too much to keep sorted out.

I dropped a huge stack of green pages and they spread across the floor.

"Fuck me."

I crouched down and carefully began gathering them up, trying not to crease the paper. I didn't need The Powers That Be thinking that anyone but the stars had rifled through the new pages. I'd get fired for sure.

But as I was down there, I noticed a white, carbon paper memo that had fallen behind the shredder. I pulled it out and my eyes scanned the page.

"Oh hell…" I whispered. "I know what they are going to do."

I ran out of the room with the scripts I finished, almost running into several interns as I went.

"Sorry! Sorry!" I shouted, spinning around to meet their dirty looks.

Unfortunately, I was turned the wrong direction and didn't notice that I was running smack-dab into Graham.

"WHAT THE FUCK, Maggie!" he said, not even stopping to help me pick up all the papers I dropped all over the floor. Again.

I was collating them as fast as I could pick them up. "Graham, I have no time for you right now."

"What?"

There was a gleam in his eyes like he could smell the

trouble I had stumbled upon and couldn't wait to get in there and fuck it up.

"Nothing," I replied to him with some finality. "Absolutely nothing. Just some stuff. With work. I'm late."

I took off down the corridor, but I could feel him watching me the entire time. I ran into Soundstage 13 and Jeff was standing there, arms crossed, as he listened to someone talking on his headset. I thrust all the papers in his arms.

"Just a minute, Maggie!" he said.

"I quit," I replied.

"Just a second," he said into the earpiece before taking it out and turning off his walkie-talkie. "What?"

"I quit!" I replied. "I'm done. I gotta go."

"Maggie, if I don't keep you this job, my life is over," he said, panic rising in his voice.

"No! No, Jeff. You're fine. You were only ever in trouble if I got fired. But I quit. You're in the clear! Everything is going to be just great!"

"That's not—"

"That IS how it works. The elves, they are very literal. Was the deal for me to keep this job or was the deal for you to make sure I didn't get fired?"

"That you didn't get fired."

I gave him a great big grin. "There you have it! You're set. No one can fire me if I quit. You're gonna live!"

He gave a huge sigh of relief. Actually put his hands on his knees and breathed a sigh like a marathon runner after a 10k. "Thank god. You were terrible at this job."

"I know," I said. "I'm awful at it. And it is almost over."

"It is?"

"I think I've figured out what is going on, but if I am to get this favor off my back, I need to go and I need to go right now."

He nodded. "Okay. Is there anything I can do to

help?"

It was at that moment the blonde costumer turned the corner. She was swinging a crescent wrench in her hand. "Oh, I don't think you are going anywhere, Maggie MacKay. I'm pretty sure you are going to stay right here with me and watch your little life, pledged to that big, fat elf, fade away."

So she knew who I was. What did I expect? Wardrobe know everything.

She took a swing at me and I ducked. As it flew back, it clocked Jeff on the side of his head, sending him reeling. Fortunately, fauns are half goat, and getting knocked on the skull is practically a mating ritual.

She tried to take another swing, but I was there with an uppercut that bobbled her neck like a dashboard figurine. Her arms windmilled and she fell to the ground. Jeff was on her in a flat second, tying her up with tie-line. I shook my hand, because fuck it hurts to hit bone. My knuckles were completely smashed.

"Nice," said Jeff as the wardrobe lady struggled feebly beneath his hulking frame. "Ever thought about a career as an Assistant Director?"

I backed away. "Just delay Chaz for as long as you possibly can." I said and then turned to run. "Oh! And before I forget! I DID steal those earrings."

"MAAAGGIEEE!"

CHAPTER TWENTY-FIVE

I sat in my car dialing Father Killarney. "Pick up pick up pick up."

He did not pick up.

I said into the receiver. "Father Killarney, just so you know, this is what they are doing. They feed off sadness, right? It 's why everything is so terrible at the studio." I started rambling and looping, hoping he'd hear my voice. "It is why I have been missing Killian so much. Are you there? This is about the vampires of longing. They feed off of longing. All they want is to make people miserable. Don't make me miserable, Father Killarney! Don't make me feed the vampires!"

I heard the phone pick up, but Father Killarney didn't respond.

"FATHER KILLARNEY!" I shouted at him.

I heard him smacking his lips together.

"Are you there?"

"I'm here, Maggie," he said blearily.

"Father Killarney, I'm talking about the end of the world and you're sitting there barely able to pull together a coherent sentence?"

"I was taking a nap, Maggie-girl."

I looked down at my watch. "It's two o'clock in the afternoon."

"There was a poker game at Xiaoming's place last night..."

Great. I was sitting here trying to save the world and the ONE GUY I thought I could call on was nursing a hangover.

"What is it that you need?"

"I was sorting paperwork," I hissed into the phone. "And I realized what they are doing."

"And what, exactly, is it that you uncovered Maggie?"

"This entire studio is focused on making people miserable. So, their new business plan is to take the old classics and remake them in order to feed off the misery of all the fans' souls they've crushed. But there's more. They own that old amusement park, Firebrand World, in Santa Clarita..."

"I love that place..."

"EVERYONE loves that place. So, today they are releasing Legions of Space—"

"Now what do you have against Legions of Space, Maggie? I loved that movie. All of America loved that movie."

"Not THAT movie. The reboot of that movie."

"Oh." There was a pause on the line. I could hear him pouring something into a glass. I told myself it had better be an Alka-Seltzer.

"This paperwork I came across," I continued, "it was for a team of demolition experts. They are going to blow up Firebrand World."

"What?!"

"Today," I replied, looking out of my rearview window for any cops who might be unsympathetic to my chronic lead-foot syndrome. "It is part of 'rebranding'. They are showing the film in a simulcast around the globe, followed up by a press conference. And at this press conference,

Firebrand Studios is going to announce a new section of the park that will be connected to this reboot that everyone is going to hate, and then they will press a little plunger attached to some dynamite, and they are going to implode the historic part of the park on live television."

I could feel Father Killarney start to wake up. "I have been takin' our youth group there every summer for three decades."

"Exactly."

"This must be stopped!"

"EXACTLY. Imagine how angry everyone is going to be if it doesn't exist anymore. Think about how angry EVERYONE in this entire city... wait... the entire GLOBE is going to be if they tear it down."

"The Internet boards will be on fire."

"Think about all of the energy that will put out..."

"Surely they had to have pulled some permits or made some sort of previous announcement so that people aren't in the way of their explosives."

"I have no idea," I said, pushing my luck and pushing the speedometer up another ten miles per hour. "But if people die? That'd be great for them. A grand buffet of negative emotion. Whatever they do, it just feeds these vampires." I pushed my car another ten miles per hour and tried to ignore the shake in the dashboard.

"Oh Maggie..."

I could sense he was finally getting what I was trying to tell him. "Remember when my Uncle Ulrich was finally able to jump from Earth to the Other Side?" I asked.

"No. I wasn't there."

"I'm sure I told you..."

"Well, remind me, Maggie."

"He killed a whole room of people. Their life force was the power source he needed to finally open a portal. Imagine the energy that is going to be released by millions of outraged souls."

"Oh... this is not good..."

"It is not good at all. The Bringers of Light could open portals... anywhere. Everywhere."

"What is your plan for attack?" Father Killarney asked, suddenly 100% awake and totally sober.

I shook my head. "I have no idea. I'm just winging it. Man, I wish Killian was here..."

"I'll bring him to you, Maggie," said Father Killarney with finality.

"No," I said, gripping my steering wheel tighter. "If he comes, they know he will be coming to be with me. He'll lead the Bringers of Light straight to where I'm at and that's not good."

"He is a wood elf, Maggie. He has invisibility cloaks and elfin shoes. He is better at hiding than you will ever be."

"I can't let him," I said, hating myself for having to say no to the one person who I actually really needed. "I can't risk bringing him in."

"Very well, Maggie," said Father Killarney, sounding a bit like my Mom when she knew I was making a bad decision but was going to allow me enough rope to hang myself. "But I think he that he is quite capable of coming to your aid."

"Sometimes you have to slay your own dragons."

"Maggie, you already have. Sometimes slaying dragons goes better when you have a dragon slayer at your side."

I sighed. "Do you think Killian has an annual pass to the park?"

"No."

"Then I gotta go this alone. Pipistrelle maxed out my credit card."

CHAPTER TWENTY-SIX

I stood in front of the gate. I hadn't figured that the price of a day ticket would threaten my ability to get in, but sheesh. At these prices, I was surprised the park even had enough guests to witness the chaos they were about to enact.

But guests they had. People were dressed to the hilt in retro 80s space outfits and t-shirts. Everyone was wearing the merchandise. There were big signs everywhere announcing it was Legion of Space weekend and that the free showing was going to be in the Old Town Vaudeville House.

There were metal detectors lined up along the front and security guards patting everyone down. I feigned I had forgotten my wallet and walked back to my car. How was I going to get in?

That's when I remembered that I worked for the studio that was responsible for this disaster. In fact, I worked for the very director. Maybe someone I knew on the crew was loading in equipment.

I reached into my pocket and pulled out the invoice from the demolition team.

I had battled my way into vampire lairs and through time-shifting ghost boats. SURELY I could talk my way past a couple of pimply-faced teenagers manning a gate.

I began walking the perimeter of the fence, hoping that I'd see a hole or a low wall or some other way in. I guess these pimply faced teenagers had dealt with other pimply faced teenagers before, though, because there was no place to sneak in or jump the fence.

But that's when I had a brilliant idea. A genius idea. An idea so huge, no one who had ever dealt with a P.A. would even blink twice.

Twenty minutes later, I walked up to the guard gate with eight coffees and one green smoothie stacked on top of one another in cardboard carrying cases, and an invoice for the demolition team tucked underneath my arm.

"Hi!" I chirped at the guard. He had a flattop buzz cut and was wearing a bulletproof vest. I've seen Marines with less weaponry than this guy. If I wasn't in the middle of saving the world, I would have slipped him my number. "I'm from Firebrand Studios," I continued, swinging my neck so my studio badge flipped around. "I work for Chaz and I was told to bring the crew coffee and Chaz his juice."

The guard looked at me through squinted eyes. "We have coffee and juice here at the park."

"Right," I said, giving him a 'can you believe these people?' look. "But it's not the right coffee and juice. You know how he can be." I nodded to the invoice under my arm. If you are going to lie, it is important to snow 'em in a blizzard of facts. "Also, there is a problem with the invoice and payroll needs them to sign this invoice, otherwise the demo team isn't going to get paid."

The guard picked up his phone and made a call.

I, however, had already anticipated his call. I had phoned the demo team about the 'invoice issue', with HUGE apologies and said I'd be right over with coffee to make up for the hassle and to get their signature.

The guard hung up and gave me a little nod.

I was inside.

I ditched the coffees and the juice the moment I turned the corner.

This particular part of the park looked like the Old West. Hell, it seemed to be a favorite motif of every amusement park built since 1950. I had to remind myself that in 1950, they were as far away from The Wild West as we were from the 1960s. The Wild West was their Mad Men.

There was an old ghost town with miners panning for gold. There were dark rides with favorite old characters from old cartoons. Hordes of visitors crowded the place. There was something nostalgic and pure about this part of the park. It just felt like childhood and happiness. I looked down at the pavement. "Son of a gun…"

There was a reason why it felt so good here. The ground was supposed to look like a dirt road, but you can't really have a dirt road in the middle of an amusement park. Dust and dropped ice cream cones don't mix. So, the designers had put together a concrete road made up of a mix of pebbles, and half of the pebbles were moonstones. They probably looked really pretty reflecting back the light when it got dark.

Moonstones also reflect back memories. This walkway captured all the good feelings of all the visitors and shone them back at people. It felt warm and nostalgic because the moonstones made it so. And THIS was the area the Bringers of Light Shareholders, Inc. wanted to tear up to make room for a terrifying space alien apocalypse war zone.

I wanted to hate them for it, but I knew every ounce of energy I fed into those negative feelings would only make their job that much easier.

I needed to sabotage their equipment. The Shareholders needed the energy of the disappointed fans after the movie AND the devastation the fans would feel watching this quarter of the park disappear to make room for the terrible movie. If I kept the blowing-up-thing from happening, maybe that would be enough…? It was a tough call, but I was only one person.

I walked over to the edge of one of the buildings. There was a big gate that led to behind the scenes. It didn't look like it was particularly monitored, but there was no way of knowing until I went in. I cracked my knuckles nervously.

And then I heard a voice say, "Maggie MacKay. We were hoping you would arrive."

I turned. One of Firebrand Studio's original hits was a Hansel and Gretel live-action puppet movie thing. At the park, they built one of those kiddie rides themed after said classic. You sit in a car and it drives through the dark and everything is in day-glo paint and happy music plays and it's all sorts of fun for the whole family.

Only this time, hiding in the shadows of the queue, was a vampire. He smiled at me, showing of the tips of his fangs, and then ran inside following the path of the track.

I didn't have my silver stake. I didn't have my neckguard. All I had was a wooden stake stuck in the top of my boot and a gun tucked into my shoulder holster that I'd be an idiot to pull out with so many innocent bystanders around. But I knew if I didn't do something, things were about to get really dark, really fast.

I looked over to see if maybe I could get the ride operator to stop the attraction. The operator's body was leaking out of the bottom of his pant leg and there was a definite decay to his form. The vampires had replaced the operator with a ghoul. A ghoul who was mere feet away from small children and their families. I just hoped I could figure out a way to end this without freaking out the masses. Freaking out the masses would only help the emo-vamps.

Between the cars and disembarking tourists, I nonchalantly strolled into the ride via the exit. Everyone was so absorbed with the singing animals they didn't notice me.

I ducked behind a 2-D tree and looked around, waiting for my eyes to adjust. I then waited a second and ran deeper into the ride. I caught the flash of pale white skin in the black light. There was my vampire. There were families and hipsters and young children screaming with delight every time something popped out. Little did they know what was REALLY getting ready to jump at them.

"Ugh. I hate how they reconfigure the classics," I heard a guy in one of the cars groan. "They just don't match the aesthetic of what was done originally."

I saw the vampire run in front of the candy cane house towards a car filled with youngsters. I told myself this was one set of children that were not going to get eaten by any witch. I threw my stake at his heart and it landed with a thunk. He fell against the side of the house and slid to the ground, leaving a trail of vampire blood behind him. Vampire blood is normally silver, but in the black light, it looked like Ghostbuster slime.

"I don't remember that from the movie…" I heard the other person say.

"Must be a scene from the reboot."

"Looks so fake. You'd think that they would invest a little more in modern technology," spoke the nerd.

"Yeah. What is that? Blood? It's florescent green. Like, what, monsters are filled with Mt. Dew Slurpees?"

"Must be trying not to scare the kids," he said. "Kids ruin everything."

Neither of them had to worry about the children. They were all pointing and laughing at the funny vampire that fell over and left a green skid mark. I tell you, kids these days are growing up too fast.

I caught another flash of too-pale skin. There was another vampire watching me from deeper in the ride. He almost caught my eyes as I turned to look. It would have been really sucky to find myself in a thrall at this stage in the game. He turned and ran.

As I went to recover my stake, I tried to comfort myself that at least the vampires weren't hungry.

The thing, though, is that the vampires were ugly. And if they are ugly, that means they're old. And if they're old, that means they're smart. I mean, obviously not too smart. One of them got poked through the heart on a kiddie ride. But the ease to which I was following this guy and they way they kept luring me deeper and deeper made me think that this had to be a trap. Somehow they had figured I'd come to the park today, something I didn't even know I was going to be doing until just about an hour ago, and that freaked me out more than anything else.

And it turns out, I was right.

I ran into the other room. It was the candy-lane forest scene that all the kids know and love. There's a big, obnoxious musical number in the movie. It's where Hansel and Gretel eat the witch's house. The designers even piped in the smell of gingerbread.

The ride ground to a halt. The car that stopped inside the room was empty. I hated to think about what happened to whoever had been loaded into that one.

And then I heard a voice that I would recognize anywhere, a voice that sounded like glass on a chalkboard.

"Maggie MacKay," he hissed. "I'm glad you could come."

It was as terrifying as when I was a little kid watching the movie for the first time and the witch first appeared. Except, it was real. I turned around and standing in the doorway with lightning effects going off was the one vampire I did not want to see.

"Vaclav," I muttered, reaching for my gun. I knew I wasn't going to be able to draw it fast enough. I had no silver stake. I had no neckguard. This was it.

He began to wheeze and laugh. "Would you believe it, Maggie MacKay, if I said I needed your help?"

CHAPTER TWENTY-SEVEN

That was something someone like me doesn't hear every day.

My thoughts went to static as I tried to figure out how to move my mouth around words. I pointed at the empty car. "I'm not even entertaining the idea of listening to you unless you set every human on this ride free."

He rolled his eyes at me. The gawddamned head of the entire vampire clan rolled his fucking eyes at me.

"I'm serious!" I insisted. I snapped my fingers at him like Chaz had taught me so well. "Chop! Chop!"

He waved his hand and about ten minions jumped out from behind the plywood cutouts to go aid those in the ride.

As I watched the room clear out, I was really glad I had paused prior to shooting him. His minions would have taken me down like an injured antelope on the Serengeti. I kept my hand on my gun, but relaxed a little. With that many vampires, he could have taken me down at any point and he hadn't.

"They are being evacuated as we speak," he assured me, folding his long arms with his long, white fingers and their long, white nails across his black-cloaked chest. His bat-like ears were translucent against the backlight.

I gulped. Now it was just him and me. We'd tangled a couple of times, but even I knew that when the day finally came that he and I faced off in our own personal OK Corral shootout, I was fucked. Vampires have mind-control and with a guy this old, he didn't need to gaze into my eyes to flip the 'whatever you want, I'm good with' switch in my brain. Just in case, though, I made sure to only look at his forehead.

"So... what can I do for you, Vaclav? Need me to pick up the pieces of some crazy train you've wrecked?"

"I want this even less than you," he hissed at me.

"That's saying something," I replied. I motioned to the quiet ride. The animatronics were still moving, but no sound came out of their mouth. There was just the clack-clack-clack of their robotic machinery. "How about spilling the beans before I decide this little reunion should come to a natural end?"

His pointed eyebrows knit tightly together in the middle of his forehead and his mouth parted in anger just enough to show off his pointy teeth. Most vampires have just the four canines. This guy was so old, his entire mouth was sharp like a shark. "The Bringers of Light seek to bring down the boundary between the Dark Dimension and the Other Side."

"Yep," I replied. "That looks to be the shape of things."

"If they bring down the boundary between the Other Side and the Dark Dimension, they will destroy my people."

"Again, not convincing me there is anything needing my intervention at this point."

"I do not like the elfin people," hissed Vaclav, "but their existence means all of us exist."

"I'm not catching what you're throwing at me."

He hissed with frustration. "All the life force in the

universe --- the Earth, the Other Side, everything, draws from the elfin forest."

"The universe is a big place," I pointed out.

"Not as big as you would imagine, Maggie MacKay."

"Tomato... tomahtoe..."

"If the elfin queen is allowed to die, all of us die."

"Well, if all of us die, why would the Bringers of Light be so intent on ending things?"

"They believe that if they destroy the boundary between the Other Side and the Dark Dimension, they can bring the Dark Dimension to Earth, a return to the days before the Great Divide. They think that they can unite the three worlds and rule over them all. They know that the elfin queen is the only force powerful enough to stop this."

"She also happens to be caught in a state of suspended animation and is fast asleep like Sleeping Beauty behind the wheel."

"The fact she has survived at all is the only reason we have not perished."

"But I thought you were sitting there trying to take down the wall between the Dark Dimension and the Other Side and Earth..." I pointed out.

"Yes, but not this way. This way destroys the root..."

"Of the Mother Tree?" I finished for him. "Yes, I was there. I saw it."

"Yes. And without the root, the Mother Tree rots, and if she rots, we all die. I try to break down the boundary to prevent my people from starving."

"And to rule over all."

"A ruler knows not to salt the ground if he hopes to feed his people."

"Wait!" I said, shaking my head incredulously. "You expect me to team up with you to take down the Bringers of Light so you'll have a better opportunity to use my people as human juice boxes? Remind me again why this is a good idea?"

"Because your people will be alive to even be considered as 'juice boxes.'" he hissed. "If you do not help me, Maggie MacKay, we all die. The Bringers of Light, the vampires, you, me, all of us will die. They are the enemy and we must unite against them if either of us hopes to survive this coming war."

"War?" I repeated. "What if I don't want to be drafted for your army?"

"You have already been conscripted. We have been protecting you, Maggie," he informed me. There was no hint of a lie in his words. "We have been keeping you alive as you so foolishly went into the lion's den."

I needed a little more information on this front, but just managed an eloquent, "What?"

"Do you wonder why you have not been under attack? Do you wonder why your days have been so quiet and still? We have stood guard at your Starlike Apartments every night as you slept, dispatching those who would kill you. We fight side by side for as long as is necessary to overthrow the Bringers of Light. And then our partnership is over, you and I will again be enemies, and I will drink your blood until your heart stops, Maggie MacKay."

"You are not pitching this very well," I pointed out to him. "If you wanted to get my on your side, informing me you plan on killing me after all this is said and done is not helping your case."

"I have no reason to lie to you. I do what I must for my people's survival. The prophecy states that you will kill my people. And so I must protect them from you."

"Prophecies are flights of fancy made up by people's crazy mothers, usually people who couldn't accurately predict the numbers in a neighborhood game of bingo."

"The prophecy has been spoken."

"I wouldn't be so hell-bent on killing you guys if you guys would just stop trying to kill my people," I pointed out.

"We are predators, Maggie," Vaclav replied. "You ask a tiger why he does not eat the bamboo instead of the deer in the forest."

"Yes, that's what I'm asking. Especially since some of the people I love the most are those deer. Have you ever thought about going vegan? I hear it is great for the body."

"We are dead, Maggie."

"Don't I know it."

"Our skin rots. Our insides rot. Like the elves without the Mother Tree, we rot. Not because we want to, but because someone turned us. You hate me, but only because I do what I must to survive."

"Yeah. I do. Because what you do to survive involves making sure others don't survive."

"The day will come, Maggie MacKay, when your life will be bleeding from you but the fate of the world will depend upon you living. You will ask me to save your life by turning you. If I say no, it means that we all shall perish. But believe me, it will be a kindness if I kill you."

"It'll be a kindness if I kill you for insinuating such ridiculous nonsense like that I would ask you to turn me rather than letting me die."

"The day shall come, Maggie MacKay," he wheezed at me. "Be prepared for your choice. Eternal existence to save the world or death and the destruction of everything you know and love."

"I'll get right on that," I replied, dryly. "Now, if you will allow me to get going, I have a world to save. Which I was in the middle of saving when you distracted me by this little peace summit."

"The diamond earrings you stole can be used to free your World Walkers," he said.

That made me shut up. "What?" I asked, needing him to repeat what I thought he just said.

"I offer this to you as my peace offering," he replied. "We cannot attack the Bringers of Light, for the sun is in the sky. If we secured the bracelets your Uncle Ulrich promised us, we would be able to fight them."

The whole world seemed to tilt on its axis. "You wanted the bracelets in order to fight these Bringers of Light?"

Vaclav waved my question away. "You have no time for this, Maggie. Destroy the Bringers of Light. We can only fight them when they come indoors. My people are inside the buildings that will be demolished and we kill all the Bringers of Light that venture within. But you must stop them where we cannot go. You must stop them beneath the sun."

I seriously had no idea whether this was a good thing or a bad thing anymore.

"You shall need your World Walkers, the ones that have been turned into stone. Use the diamonds to cut through the marble and free them," he said.

The ride suddenly jerked to a start.

"They have found our ghoul," he hissed, backing into the candy house. "Run!"

And run I did.

But not fast enough.

Something grabbed my ankles and I fell flat onto the ground. Whatever it was sat on my back and bashed my head into the cement of the floor. The world exploded into black with little white dots. I forced myself to keep conscious. I felt someone rip whoever it was off me. I turned, struggling to my feet.

Vaclav was standing behind a man dressed like a guard. He had punched through the guy's back and now his claws were sticking out of the front of the guy's shirt like some bad horror film.

"RUN!" he hissed at me again.

I stumbled to my feet and ran out the front of the ride. I had to grip the wall. My head was pounding and the world was swimming. I stumbled towards the employee entrance, opened the gate and went inside.

And that's when they got me. Again.

A gag was shoved in my mouth and a black plastic bag put over my head. I tried not to struggle. Air was a commodity. I was knocked to the ground and duct tape was wrapped around my wrists and ankles. I was being picked up and carried away. I felt myself being dropped onto some sort of a metal platform. I felt fabric being dropped on top of me. The platform began to move and there was the hum of electricity. I was on the back of a golf cart. My time at the studio taught me that sensation. I tried to remember that my fear was a delicacy to these bastards. They wanted to crack my shell and suck the marrow of my feelings. I tried to remember what Father Killarney tried to teach me. I was a leaf on a river. I was a leaf floating by. I was a leaf on the wind. The fear made me feel like I was getting stabbed through the heart.

I kept breathing, even though the air inside the bag was growing stale. I tried to assess just how bad this was. I mean, other than fucking bad. I struggled with my bonds. I knew as soon as they left me alone, I could rip through the duct tape. I just hoped they gave me a moment before they killed me. I knew the statistics. When a person is moved to a secondary location, their odds of survival becomes about 1%. 99% chance I was going to die if I let them take me where they were taking me. I couldn't do anything, though. The bag over my face let in just the smallest bit of air around my neck. If I moved too fast, I'd suffocate. Already, the world was hot and stale.

The cart stopped and I was picked up again. We were going indoors. I was greeted by the blessed feeling of air-conditioning. I heard doors swinging open and then I was thrown down onto the concrete floor.

"Can you imagine the sort of portal your death shall create," whispered an androgynous voice. Seriously, I had no idea if I was dealing with a chick or a dude. If I was going to die, the least they could have done was let me know if I owed Graham on our bet or if he owed me.

Fingers mercifully ripped a small hole in the bag. "Let's not have you die before your time. Enjoy the show," it murmured and then was gone.

I heard his or her footsteps retreat. They were light on the ground. Sounded like long strides. It could be that my captor was running. It could be that it was some creature of air. It could be that I had found our elfin traitor. It had been strong enough to be an elf. And then I heard the door open and close.

I had no time to waste. I flipped onto my back and tried to tuck my knees up. If I could swing my arms under my feet to the front, I could break the duct tape. But they had run tape from my hands to my feet and I was getting tangled in the sticky mess. I tried to keep the peaceful calm inside of me as things went bad to worse. I couldn't panic. Not with a plastic bag over my head and me without my neckguard. I couldn't think about the fact that no one was here. Not even a fucking vampire. What the hell was Vaclav promising when he said we were joining up forces? SURELY they could help a sistah out when she was hog-tied in the middle of some dark room.

I tried to ignore the thought there could be someone out there in the dark, someone who was just remaining very, very quiet, who was enjoying watching me struggle. I was in the middle of some empty building they were getting ready to blow up. No one was going to come looking for me. My charred body would be nothing but ash.

I tried to form a portal, but nothing moved. I couldn't focus my eyes. I couldn't reach out to touch the veil. I was trapped. They knew what they were doing.

I suddenly felt hands rip the bag off my head and I couldn't help the cry of surprise that escaped my mouth.

"Shut up, Maggie," said a gruff voice.

Fuck.

It was Graham.

I wondered what I would have to do to get him to put

the bag back over my head.

I'd take my chances with the dynamite.

"I don't want to save you either," he hissed at me as if he could read my thoughts. "But SOMEONE went and got herself captured because she's a dumbass who didn't think that sometimes dressing like a security guard or a janitor is better than to come in guns blazing while dressed up like Elvira."

He yanked the gag out of my mouth.

"I do not look like Elvira," I glared at him. "I'm wearing mom-jeans and a simple black t-shirt Trovac left for me." Okay, so I ripped out the neck of my t-shirt a la Flashdance and had torn out the waistband of the jeans so they didn't sit up around my boobs. But still. Elvira?

He stared down the top of my shirt. "Coulda fooled me."

"Shut up, Graham," I said. "What the hell are you doing here?"

"I'm looking out for my own personal interests," he said. "I'm here to make sure you don't get yourself killed because the moment you get yourself killed, I get stuck here. So, consider this is just me looking out for myself."

I felt him rip the tape off my wrists. "FUCK that hurts!"

"Gotta do it fast. It'd be a lot easier if you waxed your arms like girls should."

I rubbed my wrists. "It is PEACH FUZZ," I replied. "And for the record, it didn't hurt because of peach fuzz. It hurt because you ripped the fucking skin off my body."

"Arm hair on girls is gross, Maggie," he replied.

I pushed his hands away and pealed the tape off my ankles.

"It hurts worse if you do it slow," he remarked.

"Not with duct tape it doesn't," I replied, glaring at him.

He was having none of it. He reached down and ripped it off. "And now we're done and can go save the world."

"God, I hate you," I replied.

"Aren't you going to say that I'm an 'angel sent from above'?" he asked. "Or is a little gratitude too much to ask."

"We gotta come up with a better name for what you people are. How about Assholes With Wings? Winged Assholes? Wingholes?"

"We were anointed by God, Maggie."

"Do you want me to get that for you?" I asked.

"Get what?"

"The name you just dropped."

"It ain't dropping names if it's true."

I stood up. "You are nothing but a genetic reject with wings, asshole. Quit playing the celebrity card."

"I'm merely here to do the Lord's work," he replied, leering at me.

I punched him in the shoulder. "Cut it out. There's work to be done."

"You think I don't know that? You think I don't have a clue how important this is, Maggie? You're the idiot. Show some gratitude."

"Thanks."

"You're welcome. Now, let's go burn the Bringers of Light to the ground."

CHAPTER TWENTY-EIGHT

He threw me a janitor jumpsuit. I didn't get why he got to wear the rent-a-cop clothes and I got stuck with a white pantsuit that smelled vaguely of vomit and industrial cleaner. I only caught him sneaking a peek two or three times while I changed, so even a pig like Graham was turned off by my ensemble.

"I should have given you the cop outfit," he grumbled.

"This was your choice," I pointed out.

"Remind me next time you get the cop outfit. Or the nurse outfit. Or the parochial schoolteacher outfit."

"You are so gross. How the fuck did you get to be called an angel?"

"Life is hard when you have a reputation you don't deserve."

"Or," I offered, "you could grow up and pretend like it is a reputation you are worthy of."

"Don't go throwing that at me. I didn't ask for this."

"Such a huge fucking cross you bear."

He looked towards the sky. "She knows not who she blasphemes."

I looked up, too. "Actually, I do. And I'm pretty sure

you're siding with me in this disagreement." I zipped up the suit with finality and grabbed the rolling trashcan. I pointed at Graham. "You owe me so big, Winghole."

"Are you kidding, Maggie? I'm pretty sure you owe me coffee runs for this favor."

"Shut up, Graham," I said, flinging the door open and walking, blinking, out into the sunlight.

There were all sorts of fucking happy families with their bastard children, running around all joyful and like this was the best day of their life. Let me tell you something, my family never took me here, and I grew up just fine.

"Smile, Maggie. You're going find yourself with a manager coming over to find out what your fucking problem is."

"I hate you so much, Graham."

Graham shielded his eyes with his hand and gazed in both directions. "Where is this land we're looking for?"

"How should I know? I've been here, like, once."

He looked at me incredulously. "How can you have lived in Southern California and not come here more than once?"

"My family was broke, Graham. We were broke."

"Or maybe your parents didn't love you."

I punched him in the arm as hard as I could.

"Ow!" he said, rubbing the muscle. "I'm reporting you for surly behavior."

I looked around and saw that a bunch of the families were looking at us like this wasn't a part of their normal, everyday existence. "What are you looking at?" I snapped.

A wife grabbed her husband's arm and pursed her lips before dragging her family away.

"Ease up, Maggie-girl," said a voice behind me. A voice I recognized. A voice that was as welcome as a cool breeze on a hot summer day.

I turned around and felt like I could weep.

Killian.

Muthaeffin' Killian.

That exiled elf was supposed to be responsible for keeping the entire elfin race alive while his queen died, not standing right behind me. I ran over to him and flung my arms around his neck. And then socked him in the shoulder.

"What the hell are you doing here?" I said. "You're supposed to be in charge of maintaining interdimensional order."

"I believed there may have been need of my presence," he replied, with a strange look at Graham.

"Good thing your boyfriend got here, Maggie," said Graham with a smirk.

"He is not my boyfriend," we replied in unison.

Man, I loved this guy. I turned back at Killian and smiled. "I'm glad you're here."

He took me by the elbow and steered my garbage can around the corner as Graham trailed behind. "So, what is the plan, Maggie? Besides drawing attention to yourself and luring every bounty hunter this side of the border to you?"

I lowered my voice. "It's the studio. So, they've created this reboot of this movie that America... hell... the world loves. They rebooted it, specifically to make it awful. Today, they are not only screening the premiere of the reboot, the Shareholders are blowing up the historic part of this park to build an alien-apocalypse-themed land in its place."

"Why would they do that?"

"Because they are an organization of vampires who eat feelings."

"What?"

"New breed," I explained. "Also, it appears I'm working with Vaclav for the moment."

"WHAT?" said Killian, gazing at my eyes. "Are you Maggie? Have you been replaced by a doppelganger?"

"I'm me," I said, batting him away. I gave him the full

rundown of the emotion vampires and the blood vampires and the plan to tear things down and how that would just destroy everything.

"Are you sure it would destroy EVERYTHING?" asked Killian. "I mean, could Vaclav be lying to you in order for you to destroy his enemy?"

I rubbed my forehead. "Oh hell, Killian. It's been so crazy. I don't know…"

"He's not," said Graham, coming to stand next to us. "These bastards are bastards and they need to go down."

"And you are trusting this creature's word?" Killian continued, hooking his thumb towards Graham.

"All I know is that they are going to try to create a permanent portal right here in this park as soon as the movie stops screening and I need to make sure that doesn't happen. Everyone who is here, all these people filled with happiness and longing? They're going to see something they love destroyed. And those feelings of sadness, on top of their disappointment about this film, is going to create a hole through the boundary."

"Oh," said Killian looking around. "So, you were yelling at the families to ensure that their experience of happiness was not so high that it would dip to a devastatingly low?"

"No. They were just assholes."

"Maaaaggie…" he said to me with a disapproving look.

"Well, they were."

Killian looked at Graham. "So, what was the plan."

"We were just going to wing it," Graham said with a shrug.

Killian looked at me. "Wing it?"

As if to emphasize the brilliance of his idea, Graham unfurled his wings.

"Maggie, you are very fortunate that I have arrived," said Killian dryly.

"You're tellin' me."

"Right," he said, rubbing his hands together. "Well,

shall we go to the theater and first rid it of the celluloid that shall cause this impending doom?"

"Sounds like a better plan than what we had," I said, throwing a look back at Graham.

"Having a plan is a lousy plan!" he shouted at us as we walked away.

I couldn't help but reach out and give Killian's hand an appreciative squeeze.

"Get a room!" Graham shouted.

"Also," I said to Killian. "Vaclav told me the earrings I stole could free the World Walkers, but I left the earrings with Xiaoming."

Killian smiled. "Well, are we not fortunate, indeed? For Xiaoming visited me in the elfin forest just a few days ago to return an artifact that had been stolen from us." He reached in the sleeve of his tunic and pulled out the very frickin' earrings we needed. "I have been told that on Earth, diamonds are a girl's best friend."

"No, Killian," I said, taking them from him. "You are."

CHAPTER TWENTY-NINE

We got to the theater. It was a freestanding building. From the outside, it looked like the designer was riffing on an old vaudeville house or something. The front doors, while quite solid metal, had been painted to look like western saloon doors. On either side were movie posters. It was covered in faux-wood boards and had an upstairs balcony where the stars of Legions of Space were sipping sarsaparilla and waving at the crowd.

Firebrand Studios had used this movie house to premiere their movies since the park opened. It was one of those SoCal traditions. I mean, there was the big red carpet event down at Grauman's or whatever, but then they also held a screening here for the fans. Judging from the way the line wrapped up and down the block, I was guessing many of them slept out overnight to get their place.

"Why would you pay $100 to get in and then spend your entire time waiting in line to go sit in a dark room when there are perfectly good movie theaters in Los Angeles?" I muttered.

"The way movie ticket prices are going," said Graham,

"This might be a discount."

"Ha ha," I replied, barely giving him a glance. "So, what is your plan, Killian?" I asked.

"I believe at this point, we are just 'winging it'," he replied.

"Come on, Killian," I said. "Don't let Graham win."

He looked at the building. "Well, I suppose we could go in."

"That seems like a great idea."

I got up and started walking towards the door.

"HEY!" shouted a woman.

I turned around and looked at her. Her face was beet red. "We have been standing here for twelve hours. The back of the line is that direction."

I pointed at my uniform and Graham's uniform. "We work here."

"But he doesn't," said the woman pointing at Killian.

I looked at Killian, dressed in his tunic and tights, and then looked at her, dressed in her space suit and holding every space themed souvenir they sold in the park. I needed her to cut it out with the negative feelings. In fact, judging from her reaction, there was someone sucking on her right now. But the best way to turn her frown upside-down? Give her a little magical treat.

I walked over to her and said in a low voice. "He has a cameo in the film. We are trying to get him up to the balcony without people freaking out. Do you think you could give us a hand? Keep this on the down-low?"

The woman's eyes got huge and she looked like Christmas had come early. It might also have been that I got a little rush of heat from Killian's direction. Sometimes the elf glamour has its purposes.

"Who is he?" she asked, a sparkle lighting up her eyes.

I waved her down like I needed her to keep this a secret. "You'll know him when you see him..." I said, giving her a wink and walking away.

Killian fell into step beside me. "What did you tell

her?"

"That you were a star."

"Did it work?"

"Of course," I said, opening the door for him. I suddenly looked back and the line was a sea of cell phones and people taking pictures of Killian. "Shit."

He looked back, too, and decided to go along with it. He gave a wave and a smile.

"Excellent plan, Maggie," remarked Graham out of the corner of his mouth. Graham stepped out in front of us and blocked everyone's view with a "stand back" police stance that would make the real cops proud as Killian and I got through the front doors. Graham followed behind.

As soon as the doors closed, he jammed the handle. "That should hold someone for a little while," he said. "Sounds like the World Walkers Association is going to be stuck cleaning up another mess of yours, Maggie."

"I'm pushing a rolling garbage can and dressed in a white jumpsuit, Graham. Do you think that anything you can point out could make my day worse?"

He pointed to a figure standing at the end of the hall.

"Remind me to keep my mouth shut."

CHAPTER THIRTY

Chaz stood in the middle of the hallway looking at his phone as he finished up his text. He gave me a disgusted glance. "I see you got that promotion you were fighting for, Molly."

Killian mouthed, "Molly?" at me. I waved his question about my name away as I rolled the can down the hall towards Chaz. I had no idea how high up he was on the food chain of the Bringers of Light. Now seemed a good time to figure that out. "Chaz, there's some serious shit going down and I don't have time for you."

"Um... excuse me? Have you seen the line wrapped around the building? I'm afraid that's the only shit anyone is concerned with until 4PM today, Miss. Thang." He gave a sniff. "Glad you're here to clean up. Some people will go to such lengths to get on the VIP list."

I started walking towards the theater, but he stepped in my way and grabbed my can.

"Chaz, I need to get inside there," I said.

"Um... no you don't. I have strict orders not to let anyone in, and I'm pretty sure that especially applies to you."

"I'm just tidying up," I replied sweetly. "Don't get in the way of me doing my job."

"The day you clean up shit, Molly, is the day I eat shit. You aren't a janitor."

"What?"

He rolled his eyes. "Your gun holster is causing your jumpsuit to bulge."

Graham looked at me and shook his head like I was the biggest idiot in the world.

"You're the one who picked this stupid get up!" I shouted at him.

"So what do you have in the can, Molly?" Chaz said. "Tear gas? A bomb? The remains of your useless life?"

"Why do you not find out?" asked Killian, before knocking him across the jaw.

Chaz's eyes rolled back in his head and he was out for the count.

"TKO?" Killian said.

I held up my hand to high-five him. "Total Killian knockout."

"When you guys finish wasting time while the doomsday clock continues its countdown..." said Graham crouching down to get Chaz's cell phone. "Would you mind doing me a favor and disposing of this guy?"

Killian got Chaz's arms while I got his legs and we deposited him into the trash can. Killian rolled him down the hallway, looking for somewhere to stash his inert body.

"What are you looking for?" I asked Graham as he furiously tapped at Chaz's phone.

"His Tinder account."

I grabbed the phone. "You seriously were looking at his Tinder account?!" I closed down the app. "Gawddamnit, Graham."

"Hey! Do you know how hard it is to find a twink with a good job?"

"No, Graham! No! We do not date the enemy we have just defeated!" I announced, drawing the line in the sand.

"Jeez, Maggie. Hell hath no fury. Listen, I'm still here for you," he replied, opening up his arms towards me. "I'm fluid."

"Graham, that has nothing to do with anything. We do not pick up dates for Friday night when there is a doomsday clock counting down!"

"It takes, like, half a second to swipe right."

"SHUT IT!"

"I can multi-task."

I pinched my fingers at Graham's mouth like I was a sock puppet telling him to shut his trap as I scrolled through Chaz's texts to see what was going on. "Okay, he was told to keep everyone except the audience out of the theater. The show starts at 4PM. Demolition is at 6PM, just after the movie ends, for maximum effect."

"Where do you think the movie itself is?"

I pointed at the ceiling. "Upstairs…?"

"You see any stairs?"

"Over here!" Killian called. He motioned towards an unobtrusive door that had been camouflaged to look like a panel in the old saloon-y wallpaper.

"I'd bet cash money that's what we're looking for," I said.

Graham strode over, opened up the door, and then he ducked as he was met with a hailstorm of bullets. Poorly aimed bullets, but bullets nonetheless.

"You shot holes in my fucking coat?" Graham shouted at the guy. "Oh, you are going down…"

He ran into the stairwell headfirst. So bullets don't do much against angels. Who knew. Not that strange, really, when you think about it. Vampires can only be staked. Werewolves bounce off anything not coated in silver. Angels… well, I don't know how you take down an angel, now that you mention it. I think you have to suck them into the Dark Dimension. It's hard to know until you kill a few.

There was the sound of a scuffle and then silence. Killian and I followed after Graham. There was a body lying on the floor. Graham gave the guy a kick to the ribs.

"Come on now," I said, placing a hand on Graham's shoulder. "He's out."

"He shot a hole in my fucking coat!"

"It's a dumb coat," I said, trying to comfort him.

"It is a GREAT coat."

"You would have been the first to be eliminated on Project Runway."

"I should have left you with that bag over your head, Maggie."

Killian looked at me. "There was a bag over your head?"

"LATER!" I said, which somehow succeeded in calming everyone the fuck down. "Let's find this movie."

The projection room was dark. In the olden days, there probably would have been a great big ol' wheel o' film spinning through the projector. Instead, this sucker was digital. The movie was going to be beamed down into the projector at the same time it was being beamed down into all sorts of other projectors around the country.

I looked through the little window in the booth at the screen. It was like it was a gigantic black hole, a vortex that no one but a World Walker could see. "There it is," I whispered.

"What?" asked Killian and Graham at the same time.

"The vortex," I replied. "This is where the portal will go." I then looked over at the walls of the theater. "Oh hells…"

"What is it?" Killian asked, knowing that sometimes when I swear, it's nothing. And then sometimes when I swear it is because there is a reason a person should be cussing.

"The World Walkers," I replied, pointing over at the walls. There were niches all over the movie theater filled with the statues of my friends. "They brought the World

Walkers into the theater as decoration. But when they explode, they will enforce the portal. Their petrified bits will contain some of their magic. They're the marble reinforced concrete in this tunnel to hell."

"Come on, Maggie," said Killian, running towards the door. "Bring the earrings."

"You're going to leave me here?" asked Graham, looking a little pouty that he was being left behind. "We need to get this projection booth torn apart before someone comes looking for their friend here and sees that he isn't going to be reporting to work tomorrow. Come on. Let's destroy the projection booth!"

I looked at Graham. "You didn't kill him, did you?" I asked.

"Just put him to sleep. Now, are you going to help me destroy this projector or what?" He looked like a little kid on a playground asking the other kids to play kickball with him.

I pulled the fire extinguisher from the wall and tossed it to Graham. He caught it in his arms. "Use this to bash things in. I'm sorry, Graham, but we gotta go save the world."

"Will destroying just one projector be enough?" asked Killian. "You said that this thing was going to be a global release."

"I don't know," I shrugged.

Graham looked resigned to the fact he was going to miss out on buddy-time. "I'll destroy this projector and then fly around and destroy the rest of the projectors I can find. You destroy the construction equipment."

"Will you have enough time?" I asked.

"Well, I'll do what I can fit in before cross-fit."

I wouldn't have put it past him to actually abandon our world-saving to get to the gym, but figured we didn't have much choice at this point. He did save my ass within the past thirty minutes, so I'd give him the benefit of the doubt.

"How should we destroy a yard full of construction equipment?" I asked Killian as we started heading towards the staircase.

"Wing it, Maggie," said Graham, laying into the projector with the fire extinguisher.

"OR!" interrupted Killian. Graham and I both turned to look at him. Killian pointed at the wall. "You could rip the electrical cord out of the machine. That would also break it."

Graham and I looked at each other, feeling a little stupid about it all. I mean, in my defense, why go for effective when destructive is so much more fun.

But Graham took the advice, walked over, and yanked the cord out. It ripped out of the projector, still sparking. "That works, too."

"Have a glorious time," Killian said to Graham, then turned to me. "Now, Maggie, Graham seems to have this under control. Perhaps we should do our part to save the world?"

He ran out into the hall. I patted Graham on the shoulder. "Thanks."

He shrugged. "You can fuck me later."

"I don't think so," I replied, turning the pat into a punch and then chased after Killian. "I hate that guy."

"I still cannot believe you would join forces with him," Killian muttered, like I should know better.

"You sound like my mother."

"She would be disappointed in you, Maggie."

"He saved my life," I pointed out.

"Are you sure he is not the one who put you in harm's way?"

"Are you jealous, Killian?" I asked with a grin.

Killian looked at me from the side of his eyes. "I am sorry we cannot continue this conversation. I am running right now."

"Aw, Killian," I reassured him. "He doesn't throw a punch like you."

Killian's mouth cracked into a minuscule smile he tried hard not to let me see.

"I promise, he didn't once pull out any magical rod."

"You are just trying to make me feel better," he replied.

"Negative feelings only feed the vampires, Killian."

"Very well. I shall allow the feelings to pass."

I walked into the movie house. I could feel the thinness of the veil just behind the movie screen. It gave me the shivers.

I walked over to the first niche and Killian laced his fingers for me to stand in. He pushed me up and I got into the niche. I had to steady myself and almost knocked the statue out. I grabbed her and waited for her to stop wobbling.

"Stay steady, Maggie," said Killian.

I pulled the earrings out and looked at them in my hand. "Come on, work," I mumbled under my breath. "You gotta work."

So, the thing about diamonds is that they are the strongest substance on earth. A diamond can cut anything and only a diamond can cut a diamond. And those earrings that bitch left in her hotel room happened to have a little extra cutting power. The way the earrings were set, the pointy end of the diamonds stuck out of the back of their platinum prongs. In my hand, I could focus my portal making abilities through the facets of the diamonds and aim the energy into the tips. I held the earrings up to the statue's face and then stroked the diamond down into the marble.

It created this line of light through the stone. I cut a full circle and peeled away the rock. The woman's face was revealed and she gasped for breath. I swiped the diamond around her arm like I was tracing the sleeve and then peeled it off, freeing up her arm.

She looked completely confused. I did the other arm so she could watch and see how it works. "I don't have time to tell you everything," I said. "But, watch. You just focus your energy and it breaks the enchantment."

I continued cutting her neck and shoulders free as she spoke. "The last thing I remember was Stan..." she gasped. "He called me into his office to review my record. He said to turn around and that's when I saw her. I couldn't close my eyes fast enough. She was standing right there. The Medusa."

We had a witness, a witness who could testify. If I wasn't so hell-bent on stopping the Bringers of Light before they brought hell to Earth, I might have paused long enough to give her a hug. But I needed to get her out of the marble. "We're going to need you to be a witness against him. We're going to take the bastard down. And if for some reason things are so fucked that we can't by legal means, I swear by all that is holy, we won't let that stop us. We'll get him for what he did to you... for what he did to all of us." My voice caught in the back of my throat as I thought of the World Walkers the studio blew up and filmed. "We'll get all of them."

Now that she could move everything above her shoulders, she was able to manage a nod.

I put the earrings in her hands. "I need you to free the rest of the World Walkers," I said. "There's a vortex here. They're trying to tear down the boundary. My partner and I are going to Old Town to try to stop the wrecking equipment. Join us there. I am going to need your help."

And with that, I jumped back down to the ground. I wished we could have stayed to offer words of comfort and support as the World Walkers pulled themselves out of the rubble of their violation. But the collapse of existence waits for no one, and Killian and I had to be off.

CHAPTER THIRTY-ONE

We ran over to the oldest part of the park. Several slightly grumpy employees were ushering people out of the area and putting up a tape fence to block off the buildings. There was a stage set up over to the side where I think they were expecting Chaz to talk about the new vision of their monstrosity. Too bad they didn't know he wasn't going to be showing up. I recognized a couple of teamsters from the studio who were setting up the equipment for the live feed, and I flashed them a weak smile. I pulled Killian aside and waited.

"Any ideas?" he asked me

"The explosives are probably being laid out..." I muttered. "It is just a question if they have heavy equipment, too."

Killian looked around. "The buildings are so tall in this area, they could have hidden great machinery behind them and we would never know."

I bit my cuticle. "I am just betting something's there." I pulled out my phone and texted Jeff. "This had better work," I muttered under my breath. My phone buzzed again and I smiled.

"What?" asked Killian.

I strolled over to one of the teamsters who was setting up lights. He put down his equipment and walked away.

"What did you do?" Killian asked again, watching as man after man pulled his phone out of his pocket, put down whatever he was doing, and walked away.

I showed Killian. "I had Jeff tell everyone the union just called a work stoppage on this project. Safety concerns."

Killian gave a low whistle.

I watched as employees went running after the teamsters to figure out why they were packing up to go home. I smiled. "The World Walker Association could learn a thing or two from them."

"They will not be angry when they learn of this deception?"

I shrugged. "What deception? Firebrand Studios was about to put them in the line of fire of a hellhole. That ain't union regulation. You do NOT fuck with the teamsters."

Killian stepped aside as a burly man walked by with a cart full of equipment. "So, we have disrupted the broadcast. We have disrupted the screening. Is it enough?"

I looked at the old village. "They can still blow this place to smithereens or tear it down with a wrecking ball. I just don't know how much angst they need to put this plan into motion."

I felt a small hand on my leg. I thought it might be a lost child thinking I was his mother, but when I looked down, there was Pipistrelle.

"Pipistrelle!" I exclaimed. "How did you get here?"

"I drove a grip truck!"

I didn't even want to think about the fallout caused by a whole truck disappearing with thousands of dollars of filming equipment and then magically showing up at the park.

Pipistrelle kept chattering on. "You quit the job and so I quit the job!" he replied with a big grin. "I would not make smoothies for anyone other than the Mighty Maggie MacKay!"

"Um... thanks!" I replied. I pointed to the old village that was now completely cleared out. "So... we have to save the world. Want to go get yourself a churro or some popcorn or something?" I offered.

He suddenly pulled a huge stick of dynamite from behind his back. "I'm helping!"

I grabbed it from him before he blew himself up. "What do you think you're doing?!"

"I went through the first building and took away all of the explosives while you were freeing the World Walkers!" he replied in his squeaky little voice. "That way, you would not need to worry about the explosives. I shall create a pile and then you can put it anywhere you would like!"

I looked at Killian and he looked at me. "Um... keep doing what you're doing, Pipistrelle...?"

He gave me a smart little salute and then ran under the tape and into the old village.

"It's like we have a team of people just taking care of things while we were busy," I remarked.

"Funny how that happened," he replied with a smile. I was starting to get the distinct impression that maybe Killian made a call or two to our members, himself.

I smiled. "That just leaves us with the heavy equipment," I said, folding my arms and scanning the tops of the buildings for a shadow of anything that might alert us as to where things were. "Now, if you were going to destroy people's dreams, how would you come in like a wrecking ball?"

Killian pointed to the fairytale castle.

CHAPTER THIRTY-TWO

We stormed the castle. Quite literally. The space outside the roped off area the teamsters had abandoned was in chaos as everyone tried to figure out what the hell they were going to do now. Killian and I sprinted in and tried our best to hide as we could. There was a gate to the employee behind-the-scenes area, but it was locked. I think they didn't want people running in and getting in the way of the construction equipment, like Killian and I were trying to do. But since when has a gate stopped a full-frontal assault? I mean, other than a lot of times through history. But those castles weren't made of fiberglass and those gates weren't made of plywood. Killian again put his hand out for me to step on.

"Ladies first," he said.

"I'll let you follow behind and finish off my sloppy seconds," I replied, stepping onto his interlaced fingers.

"I shall watch your back and prevent an attack from behind."

"You just want a good look at my behind," I said as he launched me into the air. I caught the top of the fence with my fingertips and pulled myself up.

"Who would not?" he called from below. "Those matriarchal jeans are quite flattering to your figure."

I managed to flip him the bird before I flipped over the top of the gate. Sure enough, it had been bolted, but nothing I couldn't handle. I opened up the gate and Killian strolled in.

"No attacks from the rear," he informed me.

"Fantastic."

Behind the castle, it was just a parking lot. There were a couple buildings, but otherwise, just blacktop. A couple of BLAA OSHA signboards touted, "If you see something, say something" and "Let HR know if you pass out from the heat while on-duty." I guess off-duty, you were on your own.

But there was the equipment we were looking for. A crane with a wrecking ball, a couple bulldozers, a dump truck, and some bobcats to round things out.

Killian pulled a soda out from his jacket pocket. "Would you like this now or later?" he asked.

"Where did you get that?" I wondered, looking at him in amazement.

"Maggie, do you forget I have worked with you and illegal portals before? I stole it from one of the carts while you were speaking with Pipistrelle."

"Well, what do you know," I replied. "My own private medic." I was touched that he had thought of such a thing. I was an idiot for not thinking of it myself. I took the can, popped the top, and chugged it down.

I let out a massive belch.

"So, you are opening up the portal that way?" Killian asked.

"Just about," I replied. I stretched out my fingers and wiggled them in front of me. "Let's do this."

I ripped open the portal beneath the crane and watched as the tear widen. I had no idea where we were in relation to the Other Side. "Boy, I hope no one lives beneath this portal…"

The hole continued to tear open beneath the treads of the wrecking ball. It fell through as if in slow motion. I felt like I was going to throw up. The portal was so huge. Gravity was on my side, but it wasn't fun. Killian wrapped his arm underneath my shoulders and held me up.

"Keep going, Maggie," he whispered.

I swallowed down the bile and reached out my hand, widening the portal even more. The next machine fell through, and then the next.

The energy of the border called to me. It pressed on me like I was 100-feet below water. It crushed against my skull and I thought my brain was going to implode like a watermelon in a vice grip. I couldn't catch my breath. My lungs had no more air. When I had pulled my dad out of the border, it had looked thick and wide and the edges were rainbow colored like an oil slick on water. And the whole world looked like that to me. All I had to do was fall into it. All I had to do was let the border swallow me up. I didn't know if it would make it stop or make it continue forever, but I was hanging onto the earth like a mountain climber with nothing but her fingernails gripping onto a cliff edge.

"Close it up, Maggie!" shouted Killian. "Close it! You are fading!"

I screamed out. Or would have screamed. But there was no air. Instead, it was as if my insides were coming inside-out through my mouth.

And then I felt the blow as Killian popped me in the nose. Then black.

***

"Maggie?"

The world was hazy and gauzy. I think I was on the ground. I looked up at Killian. His blonde mane was lit like a halo around his head. He smiled, and it warm me to the core.

"I'm so glad you're here," I whispered to him.

"I would never leave you to face something like this by yourself," he replied, slowly stroking my hair. "You mean too much to me. I would leave the entire elfin kingdom to be by your side. Stay with me, Maggie. Stay with me forever."

And then he lowered his mouth to mine…

And a pain shot through my heart.

I woke up gasping.

Killian was leaned over me, giving me mouth-to-mouth. My ribs felt like they were on fire. I realized that as he tried to get my heart started again, he must have cracked them.

I rolled over to the side to catch my breath, which was a whole other level of hell. There was a metallic taste in my mouth. My nose hurt.

But then I noticed a ring of fifty World Walkers around us. Their hands were focused upon the rift I had created, palms outstretched as their energy hummed.

Realizing I was alive, several of them looked at me with a little bit of fear. I wanted to pretend like it was respect, but it was fear. Opening up a rift that size opens up a can of issues. Despite Killian and I saving their gawddamned life, they did not look particularly pleased.

But I had ninety-nine problems, and fifty cranky World Walkers were only forty-nine of them. I wiped my mouth. Red cracked and flaked onto my hands. "YOU PUNCHED ME IN THE NOSE?!" I croaked at Killian. "You gave me a bloody nose?!"

"You would not stop, Maggie," he explained apologetically. "I had to stop you."

I looked over at where the heavy equipment had stood. The scar from the portal was ugly. It was going to be a weak spot in the boundary for centuries, which fucking sucked.

"I didn't get a chance to heal it right," I said, reaching out with my fingers and letting my gaze soften, trying desperately to undo the damage. My hand trembled as I tried to join the other World Walkers in fixing the hole. I couldn't hold it up. There was nothing. I had tapped myself out.

"Fuck," I said, weeping, except I was so drawn down I didn't even have tears left in my ducts.

Killian gathered me up. It hurt so bad I couldn't help but cry out. "Shhh… shhhh… Maggie. You will heal it later."

"Every gawddamned demon living on the Other Side is going to come through this hole and it is my fault because I couldn't figure out a better way to get rid of a bunch of heavy equipment."

"You did the best you could."

"It isn't enough, Killian. People are going to die because of me."

"They were going to die if it wasn't for you."

"That's beside the point."

He brushed back my hair and laughed. "Think of it as job security, Maggie. You are going to be very, very busy here on Earth for a very long time."

"It's not over," I said.

"It's over," he replied.

"The fat lady ain't singing."

And then suddenly, I heard a wailing chorus of angry women. "WHAT DO YOU MEAN THE MOVIE IS CANCELLED!"

"Thank god for Graham," I said.

"I would not go that far."

CHAPTER THIRTY-THREE

Killian sat on the curb beside me outside the Starlike Apartments. His elfin jalopy was parked at the curb.

"Thanks for coming out to help," I said.

He took my hand and pressed his lips to the back of it. "Always, fair lady."

I smiled. "Admit it. You came for the opportunity to knock me out."

"Always."

I laughed. I still hurt like hell. It felt like I had been beaten every direction since Sunday. Every joint in my body ached and it felt like I was getting stabbed every time I breathed. But it was worth it. The show had not gone on. The studio was in major trouble for stealing what amounted to millions of dollars worth of equipment and the non-Light Bringing associated stockholders were firing everyone they could find associated with the plan. The angst would still feed the emotion vampires, but not at a global level and the boundary between Earth and the Other Side remained.

And you know what? People actually liked the reboot, so that didn't go as planned, too. Turns out Chaz wasn't as awful a director as the studio had hoped for. I mean, he was AWFUL. But he got it so wrong, he got it right. People were going wild for the "ironic satirical comedy remake" he had unleashed.

"Are you coming home?" Killian asked.

I still didn't know who was at the head of the Bringers of Light association. I still didn't know if Vaclav was playing me or if he had been sincere in his offer. I think Graham was on our side. At least he had done what he had said he would do.

"My favor has been fulfilled to Trovac," I replied. "But the Bringers of Light know I had something to do with this. They know I'm here, so I'll have to ask Trovac to hide me again. Which means I'll owe him another favor."

"Do not give him another favor," said Killian. "Come back with me."

I looked at him, so grateful for his support. There were certain realities, though. "What if I bring trouble to your door?"

He held out his hands. "Maggie, wherever you go, trouble will find YOU. It is a fact of life as real as any law of nature. So, leave Earth. At least on the Other Side, the people that know you and love you are strong enough to have a fighting chance."

I flipped over Killian's arm and traced the rot that was making its way through his veins. "Really? Stronger?"

"I would much rather you be close at hand. You cannot run and hide forever to keep those you love safe. They know who we are. They know where we live."

"Well, at least they don't know where I live," I pointed out, looking for the bright side.

"You really should not have burned down your house," he mentioned.

"I wasn't PLANNING on it."

"Stay with me in the elfin forest. Help me find out who is our traitor. Help me search our ancient texts," he urged. "There is a cure for our queen somewhere. If we can find it, she can stop these Bringers of Light."

I sat there and watched the sunset for a few moments in silence as I mulled things over. "Okay," I finally said. "This apartment only has a wall A/C unit, anyways."

He wrapped his arm around my shoulder and gave me a squeeze.

"Ow."

He loosened his grip. "Thank you."

I rested my head on his shoulder. "What should we do tonight, Killian?"

"What we always do, Maggie," he replied, pressing his lips to my temple. "Save the world."

What a Hollywood Ending.

ABOUT THE AUTHOR

Kate Danley began her writing career as an indie author in 2010. Since then, her books have been published by 47North, she spent five weeks on the USA Today bestseller list, has been honored with various awards, including the Garcia Award for Best Fiction Book of the Year, and her Maggie MacKay series has been optioned for film and television development. Her plays have been produced in New York, Chicago, Los Angeles, and Houston. She has over 300+ film, television, and theatre credits to her name, and specializes in sketch, improv, and Shakespeare. She wrote sketch for a weekly show in Hollywood and has performed her original stand-up at various clubs in LA. She learned on-camera puppetry from Mr. Snuffleupagus and played the head of a 20-foot dinosaur on an NBC pilot. She lost on Hollywood Squares.

Coming Fall 2016!

Book VII: Maggie Reloaded

Maggie MacKay: Magical Tracker Series

Maggie for Hire
Maggie Get Your Gun
Maggie on the Bounty
M&K Tracking
The M-Team
Maggie Goes to Hollywood
The Ghost & Ms. MacKay (exclusive to the
Nightshade Anthology)

www.katedanley.com/maggie.html

Made in the USA
Monee, IL
03 March 2023

29104037R20108